MAY WE ONE DAY PICK ALL THE SHRAPNEL FROM OUR HEARTS

SHAENRAYCE LEIGLAND

TP

TAILWINDS PRESS

Tailwinds Press
P.O. Box 2283, Radio City Station
New York, NY 10101-2283
www.tailwindspress.com

Published in the United States of America
ISBN: 978-1-7328480-8-5
1st ed. 2020

May We One Day Pick All the Shrapnel From Our Hearts

1

I returned to my childhood home after an absence of many years. My mother had broken her hip after falling down the stairs and needed somebody to take care of her. I went alone; my wife and daughter stayed in the city. Bringing them would have caused too much confusion, as I had never told my mother that I was married.

Things were much better between us. She didn't criticize me for mumbling when I talked or complain about my secondhand clothes. She didn't declare herself a terrible mother in order to get me to assure her the opposite was true. Mostly, she talked about her mother, my grandmother, who had suffered from advanced dementia, and how her death two years prior, however heartbreaking, had set my mother free. When she said that, I thought that we all bore the burdens and disappointments of our parents on our shoulders and that it was a good thing that people died, else the youngest among us would suffocate under ten thousand years of sadness.

Still, some chasms are not easily crossed, and most of the time that I was there, we did not talk. I think we both instinctively knew that the more time we spent near each other, the sooner we'd dig up old graves. So, I spent most of my time downstairs reading a book or simply sitting in the living room, waiting for the sound of her coughing or moans to get me to check on her.

Many times, she insisted I go out and explore the town. She said a man like me shouldn't be cooped up all the time. Perhaps I might run into an old friend. When I asked what she knew of my old friends, she could not remember anything about them. I remembered little as well. I suspect that she still hoped I would meet a woman. I again suppressed the urge to tell her about my wife. I knew that, given my mother's politics, she would not approve. I only half-obliged her, taking short walks around the block with my ears strained to hear if she called. It was only after three weeks of boredom that I went into the small downtown of Missoula, Montana, and sat in a coffee shop until it got dark. Then I went into the Oxford Saloon, ate a burger, and drank my first beer in seven years. The beer was cold and tasted good. I watched some of the patrons play poker until midnight.

When I got home, I heard the ringing of a tinny bell. The bell had come from my grandmother's extensive collection of porcelain miniatures. I had given one to my mother to use, but she had rejected it. She didn't want to treat me like a servant. I don't recall her ever using it before that night. I did not answer the summons right away. My mother was right; it was unpleasant. I lit a fire in the fireplace. But the ringing didn't stop, so I went up to check on her.

In her bedroom, I found her snoring over the static of the television. If she was asleep, I saw little reason to be there. I clicked off the television and turned to leave.

She called out my father's name.

—No, it's just me, mom. I'm sorry to wake you.

—Bridger?

I nodded, and then, realizing that she probably couldn't see me in the shadows by the door, said yes.

—Have you seen your father?

I stood still, wondering if I was going to lose her to her mother's disease.

—No. He's been dead for over ten years.

—That's right. Sometimes, when I'm half asleep, I

forget.

My mother's head lolled on her fragile neck. Her chest heaved in ragged breaths and the moonlight pouring through the curtain glistened off the sweat pooled in the hollow of her neck.

—Can you get me some water?

I moved to the night table, poured a glass from a pitcher of room temperature water, and handed it to her. It nearly slipped from her bony, arthritic hands.

—I'm sorry I took so long to answer the bell. I was out.

—I did not ring the bell. I know you don't like it.

—You don't have to stand on pride. I didn't come no matter how much you coughed, so you rang the bell. I'm sorry.

—I did not ring the bell.

Foreseeing no victory from this argument save a Pyrrhic one, I backed down. She handed the empty glass back to me. I poured more water into it, but she waved it off.

—I married the wrong man, she said with a sigh.

—Don't say that. Father was a good man.

—Do you think? Do you have many good memories of him?

It was true that I was not fond of my father. It had

taken me a long time for me to be able to admit that. She was right that I did not have many good memories. Not that I had many bad memories of him, either. He did not stray from my mother; he did not stay out all night. He spent most nights after his shift at the now-defunct paper mill watching television or reading the newspaper. He was there, but never could he be said to be truly present.

—It's just that he was the only man I didn't meet through my parents, my mother said. —If you were a young woman you needed permission to do things. My parents sent me to church socials and mixed Bible study groups. I had many awkward conversations with nervous young men in our living room. Their parents and mine would make some excuse to leave us alone, but I knew they were always listening at the door to see if we were getting along. I never told you about the day I met your father.

—You did. He was working as a roofer. He cut his hand and needed a bandage.

—I didn't tell the *whole* story. My parents were at a retreat. The contractors had a cancellation, so started work a few days early. Had my parents known strangers were coming when I was alone, they would have driven through the night to get back home. Your father ripped his hand open on a nail and came in seeking a bandage. It bled a lot, but it looked worse than it was. After I bandaged the wound I asked him to follow me upstairs. He did so, not understanding why. When we got to my room, I told him to close the door behind him. Then I took off all my clothes.

—Mom, I don't want hear this.

—Your father said nothing. He left the room and I trembled with emotion for a long time afterward. Three months later, he came back. Again, I took him up to my room and undressed for him. This time he grabbed me and we made love. He came back at these irregular times—I didn't know this at the time, but he had paid a neighbor to tell him when I was alone. The first time he ever met my parents was the day when, in the living room, I announced I was pregnant with your brother.

—Mom, I *don't* want to hear this.

—Your grandfather would have killed him if I was not pregnant. I never loved him. Even in my teenage girl mind, I didn't pretend to love him. He was exciting simply because he wasn't what my parents wanted.

—There are a whole lot worse. Drunks and abusers, I said.

—Oh, I know that. I'm just saying that I only let him get me pregnant because my parents limited me so much.

My mother paused to hack phlegm from out of her lungs. She spit it into a tissue.

I was uncomfortable our relationship could be undergoing some sort of breakthrough and I didn't think I was prepared for that.

—Things are much better now, she continued. —These days a woman can live on her own. She has much more choice. Oh, some of them still choose wrongly. Some women try to save the drunks and the abusers. There's a whole lot of men with a whole lot of problems. The world is full of people like that for some reason. Then there are those whom God chose to have no one to love them. Your father, had I not invited him up to my room, would have been one.

—Didn't the fact that it happened mean that God chose otherwise?

—Your father did not deserve love. He did not deserve love because he gave none himself. You understand, right?

I did understand, but I did not tell her so. To my father, I was always the "little boy." He continued to call me that up until I left for college. I did not attend his funeral. Only my older brother, Clayton—whose life ended crashing through a pickup windshield while driving drunk on Highway 93—deserved a name in my father's eyes. I never met my older brother as I was still two months from leaving my mother's womb when he died. I believe I turned out a poor substitute.

—Some people just aren't meant to be loved, my mother repeated. —You find a man in his forties, no kids, never married, he was never meant to be loved. He was not good enough.

I flinched. My mother noticed it. The wrinkles in her face relaxed like they did when she was about to tell a white lie.

—I don't mean you, dear. There is a woman out there for you.

Again I felt the words race to my tongue. I am married, I wanted to say. I have a beautiful eight-year-old daughter. But I kept silent. My mother would not think it the truth.

We made small talk after that, although we couldn't sustain it for very long. After it had died its final death, I told my mother that she could call if she needed me, but to call loudly as I would probably be in bed. I did not go to bed, however. I went downstairs and stared into the fire until early in the morning. Although her words were those of an ill woman lashing out at the world, I could not convince myself that she had not been right.

My two weeks of allotted vacation exhausted and every sick day spent, I left my mother in the hands of a caretaker, a young Native American woman with a twisting scar from a cleft lip. I returned to the city and resumed my life, as much as was possible.

Seven months later, I received a late-night phone call from the caretaker to tell me that my mother had died. I accepted the message without tears. To tell the truth, my mother's death was as much the lifting of a burden to me as the death of her mother was to her.

She left very little in the way of assets, as would be expected of a widow gradually wasting away until nothing was left. She did leave me the house. Initially, my wife resisted the move, but I pushed until she relented.

The move was easy. Crammed into a one-bedroom apartment in the city, we found ourselves in awe at the amount of space in the two-story house. It was not a big house, but it was a strange feeling to reach out both arms as far as they could go and not touch a wall.

Finding work was a different matter. The local art museum had a sudden vacancy for senior curator by way of heart attack. The job was a great step down from her job in the museum in the city, but my wife did not complain. When I looked for work, I found little. I putzed around the house for six months before I finally called my dead brother's widow. She offered me a job at her business, driving a sewage truck.

2

Two years later, on a brisk Monday morning in October, I lay in bed trying to convince myself that I didn't have a septic tank to pump in Florence, twenty miles south of Missoula. The alarm clock glared the time: 11:45. My wife's side of the bed was empty. She woke up without an alarm at or before dawn every day. I had no such discipline. My mind kept digging its claws into the dream world for as long as possible.

As I stepped into my work pants and knotted up my boots, words of frustration flew through my mind. I would be late. My wife should have woken me. I ran through different arguments in my mind. I have heard it said that husbands and wives are supposed to fight, that they are supposed to spark against one another like flint and steel. One creates warmth from flame, not a cold stone. Yet, whenever I started a fight, she would only blink her almond-colored eyes and look away. It did not help that nowadays I only started a fight because I was otherwise too afraid to start a conversation.

In the living room, I saw my wife lying on the sofa. Her feet were bare and calloused from many hours standing on them. Wrapped around her brown right ankle was a gold anklet. Her sleeveless arms sagged under the weight of her fifty years. Fine black hairs ran along them. A book covered her face. I could not read its title. Beneath the book, I knew, was a face that still retained much of its former beauty, although many would say that it was too wide, her cheekbones too sharp, her hooked nose too reminiscent of a witch. I was lucky that sometimes she chose to turn that face towards me.

On the coffee table in front of the sofa was an oversized book on Modigliani, a long-dead painter I knew little about but whom my wife adored. Beside it was a legal notepad scrawled over with her handwriting. My wife's bosom rose and fell softly. The museum was closed on Mondays, but that didn't mean she didn't work herself ragged writing grants or preparing for the ever-present fundraiser. I doubted she meant to take this break. Sleep simply sneaked up on her. I did not wish to steal what little sleep she could get, so I left without saying goodbye.

I drove to work in my blue Chevy. Most of the other drivers parked their sewage trucks out in front of their houses, but I was not going to let everyone know that I drove a shit truck. My daughter, I thought, would be horrified if her classmates knew. Her elementary school had not yet held a "career day" at school, i.e., where a parent comes in and talks about their job. I think those are only a figment of television. I don't remember them when I was in school. Just in case, though, my daughter and I worked out what I would say. Her suggestion was that I was a part-time astronaut, a part-time paleontologist (kids have a strange grasp of big words) and a part-time spy. I decided I would say I was a truck driver and leave it at that.

Work was in the westernmost part of the city that I remembered, years before, when it was all empty land with nothing on this road save for the airport. Now every inch had been measured and cheap modular buildings smothered the land. It was as if the beauty of the mountains circling the Missoula valley frightened the developers and they needed to distract us from it somehow.

I pulled up to the iron gate and punched the passcode into the black box, then parked my car next to the office. It was a small one-story brick building with a flat roof that leaked when it rained. North of that was a large metal garage. Loud country music piped out from its cavernous door. Inside, two mechanics stood bent over the engine of a '92 International truck that Maureen, my brother's widow and my boss, still hadn't given up on. I waved hello as I walked to the office. They wiped greasy hands on coveralls and waved back.

Inside the office were two rows of desks with computers almost a decade old. Just like the truck outside, Maureen didn't like to throw things out until they were truly useless. All the desks were empty except for one with an old woman named Anna, who rarely talked to me, seated at it, and one belonging to Laura, Maureen's daughter. No one ever sat at the other desks. They were made up to look like the office was busier than it was. There hadn't been a need for more than two people in the office for quite some time.

—Good to see you Laura, I said.

She did not respond. Laura was one of those people who fought back the world with the power of earbuds. I could hear a faint buzzing sound of guitars. I reached over and popped one of the buds out of her ear.

—Hello Laura, I said.

—Shit! Don't do that!

—I'm sorry. I just wanted to say hello.

—Why do you have to say hello? You could have come in and gone, and I wouldn't have known the difference.

—I said I'm sorry.

—You don't know what you're doing sometimes, do you?

She smiled. Deep crow's feet formed at the corners of her eyes.

—I never do, I said, smiling back.

—It's good to see you. You okay?

She wore a maroon hoodie with silver lettering scrawling out the name of the local college football team, the Grizzlies. Blond hair peeked out from under the hood. Her blue skirt only reached mid-thigh. She wore tennis shoes and parti-colored socks. Her outfit was a strange jumble of comfort and sexiness, even stranger given that she was in her mid-thirties.

—What are you doing here today? I asked. —I thought you were taking time off.

—Just finishing up some paperwork. I told my mom that I did it last Friday.

—But you didn't.

—No. You're here late. I thought since you weren't here, you had the day off.

—I forgot to set the alarm. I've only got to pump the Pritchards' tank.

—Again?

—He doesn't listen when I tell him he's got to relocate the tank. I don't know what he was thinking to bury it in a floodplain. He's got to move it up the hill.

—It'd cost him a lot of money, Laura said.

—Less than having us come out twice a year to pump it out. The guy's just stubborn. He thinks he knows more than everybody, and that makes him stupid.

—Well, my mom's not complaining. It's good to have a repeat customer.

It always felt strange to be reminded that this woman was my sister-in-law's daughter. We were not related. My brother was Maureen's first husband, and they were only married a year before he took his final trip through the windshield of his pickup. Laura was still seven years away, the product of her third marriage. Laura and I were closer in age than me and my brother.

—Your mom mad at me?

Despite all the empty space, Maureen had her desk in a cramped room hidden behind panes of frosted glass. Through them, I could see her working.

Laura coughed into her sleeve and shook her head.

—No, she hasn't mentioned it. But, I'd clock in quick and sneak that lazy butt out of here just the same.

—I've been needing to talk to her.

Laura raised her eyebrows as if to say that it was my funeral and swiveled her chair back to her computer. She popped the earbuds back into her ears.

I knocked on the door to Maureen's office. I heard a noise that I thought might be a call to enter. When I opened the door, Maureen had one ear to the telephone and was hastily scribbling notes on the corner of a manila envelope. She motioned for me to come inside and then held up a finger to signal that I should wait.

Her office was cramped and had no chairs. Files smothered nearly every square inch of her desk. More hung out of the overstuffed filing cabinet in one corner. Behind her, pictures and certificates hung on the wall. Some were photos of happy customers. Others were of her personal life—a tacky shot of her and her current husband, her fourth, taken at the mall; Laura at her high school and then her college graduation. There was even one of Laura as a young girl in the bath. She wore nothing but soap bubbles and a huge grin as she held up a toy boat to the camera. I'm sure Laura was thrilled about that one. One picture, however, gave me chills. It was small, inconspicuous and faded with age. One wouldn't have noticed it if they weren't looking.

My brother was dressed in a loose T-shirt from his high school wrestling team and cut-off denim shorts. Broad sunglasses hid his eyes. His right arm was wrapped around his girlfriend, soon-to-be wife and soon-to-be widow. Maureen was still a teenager. My brother's right hand hovered over her shoulder so as not to coat her white blouse in the grease caking his fingers. Behind him, his dirt bike sat half-disassembled.

—Right after my friend took that picture, your brother wiped his hands all over that blouse, Maureen said as she hung up the phone. —Completely ruined it.

—You told me.

—I did. Yes, that's right, I did.

She took a sip of Coke through the straw of a 64-ounce plastic mug with the logo of a local convenience store on it. She sighed, took off her glasses and massaged her temples. Her hair, just a shade too red to be natural. She was a few years shy of retirement age, but I doubted she would ever retire. Her business was too important to her.

—I'm a bit busy here, so will you allow me a shot at guessing why you're here? she asked in a raspy voice.

—Sure.

—You heard that Woody's retiring at the end of the month.

—Yes.

—And that opens up a slot on the Winter List.

—Yes, I know I haven't worked here that long but maybe . . .

—Listen Bridger, I hate having to lay off half of you all when work slows down in the winter.

I opened my mouth to speak again, but she beat me to it.

—You do realize you have the least seniority of everyone here?

Again, she was too quick for me.

—Before you say you got a wife and kids, remember almost everyone has kids.

— . . .

—And before you complain about debt, know we all got that, too. The new American dream isn't a house and a white picket fence. It's making your minimum payment on your credit cards.

— . . .

Maureen sighed again.

—I don't know who's going on the Winter List. I'll let everybody know in a couple of weeks. Listen Bridger, I like you, even though you come in late. You're a good worker who doesn't have his head up his ass. So, if I can put you on it, I will. But you got a couple people ahead of you. I'll let you know when I make up my mind. Does that sound okay?

—Yes, that sounds okay.

—It's good talking to you. Now, I'd get down to Pritchard's if I were you. He's already called twice. I told him you had mechanical issues, when it wasn't nothing but your ass too broken to get out of bed. See you.

—Yes, thanks.

After leaving her office, I clocked in and grabbed my work jacket from the small locker room. I bought a soda from the vending machine and debated whether I should say goodbye to Laura. I wanted to ask her about something, but she was lost to her music again.

3

After work, I parked my car at home and walked to the health center at the University of Montana. On the front steps, my daughter bounced up and down for joy. Her bright pink backpack jumped up and down too, as if it had a mind of its own. She wore a blue winter jacket and white snow pants. Although it had yet to snow this year, and wasn't even that cold, they were her favorite pants. It was all I could do to keep her from wearing them in the heat of summer.

She did not wear a hat. I loved seeing my daughter's curly caramel-colored hair. Her eyes glittered. She stomped her black boots against the ground in her excitement. She leapt down the stairs and gripped my waist in her arms. She pressed her right thumb against her forehead and splayed out her fingers in sign language for "Daddy" again and again.

How are you, love? I signed.

Her ability to read lips was near perfect, so I did not have to fumble through the words with my fingers. I could remember the signs, but every time I used my fingers, they got tied in knots. I understood what she was saying most of the time. Now, however, in response to my questions, my daughter's fingers flew like birds in a storm, and I doubted that someone with twenty years' experience in ASL could follow her. I grabbed her hands in order to get a word in.

Where's your speech therapist? I signed.

My daughter cocked her head.

—Where is your speech therapist? I asked aloud.

My daughter shook her hands from my grasp.

Inside, she said. *She had a lot of work to do.*

I peered into the tinted glass door. When I saw movement, I rapped on the glass, unsure if it was my daughter's therapist or some other phantasm. The figure turned, seemingly deciding between answering my knock or melting back into the shadows.

The woman who answered the door was in her late twenties. Despite that, a streak of gray hair shot like a lightning bolt through her long brown hair. Pearls swung from her gold earrings. Her brown dress seemed more suitable for a nun than for a graduate student. She looked very tired.

—Thank you for seeing Eppy, Miss Janacek, I said. —I know it's not the regular day.

—Believe me, Miss Janacek said, —it's you who are helping me. I have been so busy, you know. But next week, her and I are going to meet at the regular time. Does that sound good?

—Yes, that's good.

The therapist made to close the door, but I wasn't done talking. I hooked a thumb around the door, hoping that the movement was non-threatening. Miss Janacek's eyes darted to my thumb. I leaned in and whispered, even though my deaf daughter could neither hear us nor read our lips. A squirrel hopping in a circle around the trunk of a tree with an acorn in its mouth commanded all of her attention.

—Has she been speaking? I asked. —Just you and her?

Miss Janacek lowered her eyes and shook her head.

—She has the ability, she said. —That much I know. It's just that she doesn't use it. She's getting to that age where she is beginning to really care what the other kids think of her. They laugh at her for the way she talks.

—It's just that it was so sudden, I said. —One day our house was full of her bubbling chatter. Honestly, I didn't think there was a way to get her to be quiet, but then . . . nothing.

—I don't know what to say, Mr. Bridger.

—James.

—James? Well, then call me Susan.

—No. My last name is James. My first name is Bridger. You can call me that, if you'd like.

—That's right. I remember you telling me that when we first met. Now, if you please, I am very sorry, but I must turn my attention elsewhere.

Susan the therapist nodded and ducked back into the building lobby. I sniffed the air. I thought I caught the scent of marijuana. Perhaps that was the overactive imagination of a parent, trying to search out any possible threat to my daughter. It could explain the speech therapist's lethargy. It was most likely that she was just tired from mountains of schoolwork, regular work and patient care. Still, in the back of the mind, an image burned of a drug-fueled sex party right in front of my daughter. I shook the absurd picture from my head.

—Still not talking today, kiddo? I asked as we began the walk home.

Eppy shook her head.

—Is it because the other kids are teasing you?

Eppy shook her head again.

—Is it Darren?

Eppy hesitated, and then shook her head. I knew I had hit upon something.

—He just likes you. That's why he pays all that attention to you.

I hate him, she signed.

—Hate is a very bad word.

I don't care.

—You should be nice to him. It's not his fault he's the way he is.

He's gross. He picks his nose and wipes it on his pants.

I feigned horror and disgust, and we laughed together. We watched the local football team on the practice field for a little while and then walked across the footbridge over the Clark Fork river. Our home was nearby, but my daughter's eyes looked longingly across the street to the building with the sign "Goldsmith's."

—It's too cold for ice cream, Eppy.

I know that, she signed with a sad face.

—Didn't we agree that ice cream would only be for special occasions?

Daddy, I know.

I grabbed her hand, and she gave a little squeal of delight as we crossed the street and headed toward the ice cream parlor. I was a terrible father, a fatty-fat-fat who couldn't admit that he used his daughter in order to indulge his sweet tooth. I imagined one day we would both be three hundred pounds and perfectly spherical, rolling down the street and chanting for ice cream.

We went inside and sat down at the ice cream counter. A young waiter popped his head in from the back room (where the restaurant was) and looked at us in surprise.

—You folks want ice cream?

—Yes we do, I said.

—But it's October!

—That doesn't change anything.

—Oh yes. I'm sorry. Just a moment.

He ducked back into the restaurant, and then came back to the front carrying a pair of plastic gloves and an ice cream scoop. Then he slid behind the counter and began peeling the lids off of ice cream cartons.

—How are you today? I asked. —Jack, is it?

—Yes, I'm Jack, he said, looking down at his name tag, which read "Jack." —I couldn't be better.

—You could be off work, I said. —That would be better.

—What, ha ha. Yes. Now, what is your name, Little Miss?

Eppy looked at him and then at me with panic in her eyes.

—Her name's Eppy, I told the waiter. —She's shy around strangers.

—I got a cousin like that. She's just the cutest thing when strangers come 'round. All big eyes and whimpers. It's a big act 'cause otherwise, she's a bit of a terror, always throwing temper tantrums and stuff. Not that I think your daughter's like that. Eppy? Huh. I've never heard that name before.

—It's short for Eponine, I said. —From *Les Miserables*.

—No sh–crud. I went to New York years ago, and my mother dragged me and my sister to that musical. I don't really go for that sort of thing, culture and all, but the music, it was nice. Now what can I get you? Jack said, leaning over at Eppy.

I suppressed the urge to say, "Actually, she's named after the character in the *novel*, not the musical. Do you even read?" Nobody likes that guy.

Eppy was still terrified, so I leaned over to her and pointed each flavor out to her, pronouncing each word clearly, not for her deaf ears' sake but to make it easier to read my lips.

—Vanilla?

Eppy shook her head.

—Mango?

Eppy shook her head again. Recognizing the game, Jack the waiter joined in. He worked down the line. Eppy watched him point and quickly shot her eyes up to read his lips. She rejected all flavors until we got to Rocky Road. She thought for a few moments, cocking her head to the side before nodding.

—Rocky Road it is, I said. —Okay, one scoop of Rocky Road and I'll . . . What is it?

Eppy grabbed my arm to get my attention. She held up two fingers.

—Two scoops? Eppy, you're going to wreck your appetite. Okay, two scoops of Rocky Road. No? What other flavor?

She looked at the row of ice cream tubs.

—This again? Okay. I'm sorry, I told Jack.

—Oh, don't be, Jack said through his laughter.

He worked through the flavors again until she found another that she liked.

—Are you a crazy person? I joked with her.

Eppy broke out into a huge smile. She liked this game.

—Bubble Gum? I asked. —You want Bubble Gum on Rocky Road?

She nodded her head, her smile as wide as the ocean.

—Oh no, my daughter is a crazy person. A crazy person I say.

Eppy swung her head side to side and twirled her fingers in a circle around her ears before the giggles overtook her. After the three of us had stopped laughing, I ordered a scoop of vanilla ice cream for myself. Jack prepared them. We paid, and then he disappeared into the back of the restaurant.

Eppy bit into her two scoops of ice cream, her face belying her realization that the two flavors most certainly did not go together. She put her bowl down in front of her, looked to make sure that the waiter was gone, and then began to sign.

At least I'm crazy and not boring, Vanilla is boring.

—Well, when you get to be my age, you appreciate boring. You keep on eating Bubble Gum and Rocky Road together, your tongue is going to say, "That's it!" and it's going to pack its bags and move away.

Good! My tongue will run away and become a singer. It'll be up on stage like this.

With her right hand, she wiggled her fingers, mimicking a flapping tongue. It was silly, and I wanted to laugh, but bitterness rose within me.

—You've got to start speaking again, Eppy, I said.

She stopped her puppet show. She pouted and then turned her attention to her ice cream. I knew I had said the wrong thing. All the way driving home, I had imagined her and I talking. I imagined that today would be the day that I would break through to her. Instead of asserting my authority, I had caused her to close off more. I had read many books on parenting, particularly parenting a disabled child, but all gave conflicting views and ill-advised suggestions. It did not take long to realize that they knew little better how to raise a child than I did. All that one can do is try and give that child a chance to raise themselves. One must be kind and provide a good home environment, but plenty of bad people have been raised in the best of homes. Plenty of good people have clawed their way out of the hells of drug-addled parents and pedophiliac neighbors.

This is perhaps the beauty of the human race, I suppose. A child grows into an adult and becomes a complete person. If we were all like our fathers, we would never have left the caves and would still sacrifice animals to satisfy the gods of lightning. But I wished I could teach my daughter everything that I had learned. It was sad to think about all the knowledge lost each generation because fathers could not talk to their daughters and mothers could not talk to their sons. We were stuck behind this veil of words, these meaningless noises that never quite translated anything correctly. And it was frustrating how just one phrase, one bad sentence like the one I just spoke, could hurt so much. It wasn't what I meant at all, as Prufrock said.

—Are you done with your ice cream? I asked.

She twirled her scoop around the remainder of the treat and sucked as much as she could off it. She nodded. I looked around, thought about finding the waiter to tell him goodbye, although what would be the use of that as I had already said goodbye? My daughter and I left, and I had to shake away the feeling that we were sneaking out without paying. In fact, as I stood on the curb, I flipped open my wallet to be sure that I had paid. The receipt was there. I felt that I had once again outrun my grandmother's dementia.

My daughter tugged my hand. She pointed to the sky. It had started to snow. Large flakes sailed down, and I tried to be happy, but all I could think was that it would make driving difficult tomorrow if it snowed. She tugged my hand again. I looked down at her and she smiled up at me.

4

—Out of my way, paleface, came a voice from behind me. —When are you going to stop stealing our land?

I looked over at the Native American man sitting in a mobile scooter. He wore a camouflage jacket that barely contained his girth. He had a long gray handlebar mustache and wore a Redskins cap on his bald head. A faded blue blanket was stretched across his lap. There was a dip in the fabric where his left leg should be.

—How can I steal your land, I joked, —if you never get your fat ass off it?

I grinned at the man. He laughed a belly laugh that seemed to shake the entire room. I bent down and embraced him and scooted my barstool over to make room for him. The bartender, another Native American in a flannel shirt, his long black hair tied back in a ponytail, poured a drink with well whiskey and diet soda and plopped it in front of him. Chet, the man in the scooter, dug into his coat, pulled out a wad of crumpled bills and paid for his drink.

I started coming to the Oxford saloon a few months after moving back to Missoula. My wife and I were still talking then, but not much. I hadn't been in since the day my mother told me I wasn't worthy of love. Chet had called me over to drink with him and we became friends.

It was only nine o'clock. My daughter went to bed early. I had snuck out of the house before my wife got home from her religious study group.

The bar never got busy until about 1:30, when bartenders announced last call at the neighboring bars, and college students stumbled in looking to complete their night with an order of bacon and eggs, an omelet, or "JJ's," the house specialty of a chicken fried steak in spicy sauce.

Behind where Chet and I sat was a poker table with a revolving group of players. To our left was the restaurant. The short-order cook flipped and scraped the griddle with his spatulas while laughing at something an elderly customer at the counter said. Around the corner were two rows of video poker and keno machines, which found quarters at all hours of the night. Behind a bronze set of bars, the heavyset cashier smoked in defiance of the statewide ban on indoor smoking.

—Did you catch that joke of a game earlier today? Chet asked.

—Part of it, I lied.

I never had any interest in sports, but I long ago learned that a man had to at least pretend interest. I'm sure there are many women out there who have no interest in clothing, but they feign interest to have something to talk about with other women, some idle talk to prevent true human connection.

—Sickening, Chet said. —Fucking sickening. Thirty seconds left, the Pats throw it up. Nowhere near the guy. Oh, but what's this? Pass interference? There was no pass interference. Two plays later, Pats win the game. Disgusting. After it all, the announcers are all "What an amazing comeback! This is a true champion caliber team." They're giving accolades to the players when they should be giving them to the refs who orchestrated it all.

The bartender, Mick, scoffed.

—You got a problem, Mick? Chet asked.

—How can you watch the Redskins, man? Don't you have any pride?

—Of course I got Native pride. I have no problem with the name, I just wish they'd let us Indians get a chance. An all-Indian team led by the ghost of Jim Thorpe. And, we get to carry tomahawks. Every Sunday it'll be, "He's at the thirty . . . he's at the twenty . . . he's only got one defender to beat, and HE'S DECAPITATED HIM. HEAR THE CROWD ROAR!"

—I'd watch that, I said.

Chet continued his imaginary game of football, taking revenge on everyone who ever did wrong by his people.

—"It looks like he's got quite a touchdown celebration. Is that a rain dance? Goddamnit, I left the top of my convertible down."

I walked over to the jukebox and flipped through the selection of ancient country music, not so much to find something to play, but rather to gain a small respite from the crowd, the noise and the booze. After only four drinks, my head already felt like it was underwater. I scanned the faces of the crowd. Most were regulars, men and women who had ridden the stools here for years. I was just a young man to them, despite my forty-three years. Over the weeks that I had been coming here, I had noticed a hierarchy. Each of the old-timers, as regulars called themselves, had their favorite chair. They'd sit there as often as they could. If a non-regular came in and took a designated stool, sooner or later the regular would find a way to take it back. If the newbie went to the bathroom, for example. Or another old-timer would invite the offender to sit next to them and share a drink. When I first started coming here, I fell for the second one a lot. I thought that the people here were just friendly. Even now I didn't have a set seat. I was still much too new for that, but I tried to sit at the west end of the bar, next to where Chet liked to squeeze in with his scooter.

Chet was high in seniority, but not the highest. That honor would go to Charlie. He always sat alone at a small round table in an alcove next to the front window. He was somewhere in his eighties, wore dirty Carhartt coveralls and a blue trucker's hat, and always kept his oxygen tank by his side. I had only spoken to him once, before I knew the rule that you never spoke to Charlie. He was pleasant enough, but he came here to be alone. I never could understand that. Charlie would laugh at jokes told at the bar, and a shout from the bartender of "Ain't that right, Charlie?" would elicit a response of "Yeah, I guess that's right." I envied the ability to just sit and do nothing by oneself. I think that possibly it meant that he had a greater sense of self, and didn't need external reinforcement to stay sane. I am too neurotic for that.

Next in line was Annabelle, a six-foot-two lesbian in her fifties. She stood at the east end of the bar. In the chair next to her was her most recent girlfriend. Annabelle owned a New Age shop that sold healing crystals. Her girls tended to have tattoos, partially shaved heads, odd piercings. The girl sitting next to her that night had hip-length hair dyed a brilliant blue.

The middle of the bar was taken, usually, by Smooth Bill, a used car salesman with gray hair; a couple seats over was Angry Bill, who was never particularly angry except when someone asked for the story to his missing right hand. Then he'd chew the guy out and wave his hook around. More than once, Nick had to call the cops on him. I got the story about Bill's hand from Chet the day after I made that mistake. Bill had sacrificed his hand to the mulchers at the Stone Container paper mill years ago, before it shut down.

—Get your candy ass back here, Chet shouted over to me. —None of your girly music on that jukebox.

—I only listen to manly music, I snorted back. —You know, like "YMCA" and "Macho Man."

The bar laughed, and that felt good.

—Come back here and drink your shot, said Smooth

Bill, lining up several glasses on the bar.

I walked back to the bar and smelled the liquor. Well tequila. I crinkled up my nose. Smooth Bill called over to Annabelle, her girl, and Angry Bill to take a shot with him, too.

—Don't be a pussy, Chet said.

—I'm not a pussy, I said.

Annabelle grabbed my head and licked the side of my face. When I tried to pull away, she licked again. Her breath smelled like twenty years' worth of stale cigarette smoke. It was disgusting, but her girlfriend's tittering laugh somehow made it better. When her girl moved in between me and Annabelle, I caught the look of disappointment and jealousy on Smooth Bill's face. He must have bought the drink so he'd have a chance to flirt with the blue-haired girl. That made me feel better about the well tequila. We shouted a jovial cheer and dropped the glasses back.

The night continued. Things began to mellow out. Chet switched to diet soda at eleven o'clock, and at midnight his sons came to pick him up in his van. His Native American stomach could not handle booze like us European folk. Smooth Bill left soon after and Angry Bill tried his hand at the game of poker. He lost badly. Annabelle and her girl sat without speaking to each other. I think it was something of a fight. I was a bit too drunk, tired and sick of waiting. Then the Higgins Street door opened.

I did not turn around, but happened to catch the flash of Laura's gray hoodie behind me. I counted to twenty-five, laid down enough money to cover my drinks, and walked over to the area with the video poker machines. Laura sat at the furthest one down the line. I pulled up to the machine next to hers and dropped in eight quarters.

—Don't sit next to me, Laura said. —It looks suspicious.

—It'd look even more suspicious if I try to whisper to you from four machines away.

—Then don't talk to me.

I grunted and moved two machines away, leaving my two dollars in to surprise whoever sat there next. We played our machines in silence. My bad luck kicked in as usual. After my first two dollars were gone in less than a minute, I reloaded with a five-dollar bill.

—They know me here, Laura said.

—You're worried about your reputation? We all got bad reputations here. If anything, you class up the place.

Laura cleared her throat loudly. She looked around in a panic, making sure nobody noticed her in the corner. The only other person in the casino area, a middle-aged woman with chemical red hair, was too intent on her screen to notice. I cursed as what I thought was a straight flush on my screen turned out to be missing a three of diamonds. I had saved a three of hearts by accident.

—Are you paid up? she whispered to me.

—I think so.

—What do you mean you think so?

—I'm paid up.

—Count to twenty, no, fifty, and then follow me.

Laura went out the back door without another word. I tried to follow her wishes, counting all the way to thirty-five before impatience dragged me to my feet. Passing by her machine, I noticed she still had around seventeen dollars on the machine. I printed out the ticket and headed out the back.

The back door of the Oxford opened out onto a parking lot. Laura was at the far end of the lot, breathing warmth into her gloves and jumping around in the cold. I strode up to her but before I could reach her, she turned and walked away. I had to trot to keep up.

—You left this in the machine.

She ignored the ticket in my outstretched hand. Then she took it, scanned her eyes across it, and tore it into several pieces, letting the remnants flutter to the ground.

—What the hell did you do that for? You could have at least given it to a homeless person.

She did not respond. She walked with a purpose.

—Where are you going so quickly?

She cleared her throat loudly again.

—I just want to be away from people.

—I'm people.

Laura stopped in her tracks. Such was her speed that I was still several paces behind. Although her face was half-turned away, I saw a smirk form in her smile. She reached out a hand behind her. I took it into mine.

—You're not people. You're a person. A person I can stand.

We stood there for a moment, massaging each other's hands. After a minute, she turned to look at me. There was a smile.

—Come on. I want to walk out over the bridge.

—Okay.

—It'll be cold, she said.

—Well, I come prepared.

I reached into my coat pocket and pulled out a set of ear muffs. They were bright pink and had a pair of bunny ears sprouting from each side. Laura took one look at them and burst out laughing. She laughed so hard that, as she tried to speak, she gasped for air.

—You look ridiculous, she said between coughs.

—I'll have you know, I said with a mock pout, that these are my daughter's favorite pair of earmuffs.

I had said the wrong thing. Laura's smile dropped and she strode away again. I did not know if I should follow. Talking with her was like tiptoeing through a minefield. The littlest thing could set her off. It did not help that I was the one setting the mines. I should not have brought up my family. I followed after her.

Laura stood in the center of the Higgins Street Bridge. The black water of the Clark Fork river drifted by below us. The wind was bitter cold. I walked over to Laura's side and placed my hand over hers on the rail. She did not pull away, and I considered that a good sign.

—Do you love your wife?

I was not ready for that question. I stammered out a negative.

—I do not believe you. You hesitate. You still love your wife and that hurts.

—It's not that I love or I don't love her, I said after I had collected my thoughts. —I cannot say that I ever truly loved her. We are together because accidents happen. We were never meant to fall in love, and we didn't fall in love. I tried to. I think we both tried really hard to pretend to be in love. We had a kid together, thinking that would help. Now, she's just like a cat that stays around the house, looking at me with impenetrable eyes.

—You sound like you don't respect your wife that much.

Here is what I wanted to say:

—On the contrary. It is not that she doesn't deserve me. It's that I do not deserve her. She is so great. She worked at the greatest art museums in the world. She was assistant curator of a museum in Berlin for years. She's held Picassos in her hands, do you understand how intimidating that is? And what is she doing here? She followed me here, for what reason? Out of some backward tradition that a woman must blindly follow her husband? No, things would be much better if she saw how much she is wasting her life here.

I can, at times, find the perfect words to say, but I'm always too late or unable to express them. I have wasted countless conversations like this.

—It's complicated, I instead said.

—Ugh. Everyone's so complicated. No, people aren't complicated. People just want to feel complicated. They want to feel that their life is somehow of greater importance to others. You, Bridger, are not complicated. You want to fuck a girl younger than you because you're sick of fucking a woman older than you.

I did not respond. She was right and I felt ashamed. I did not know if I should go or if I should stay.

—Listen, I do like you, Laura said. —And I'm not looking for a boyfriend or a husband. I just don't want to be used. So, if you're doing this to try and get back at your wife . . .

—No, that isn't it, I said. —It isn't it at all.

She looked up with vulnerable eyes. She wanted me to say something. If I had said the right thing, she would be mine forever. But the well had dried up. I said nothing.

—I don't think you should come up tonight, she said. —Don't be mad.

—I'm not mad. Why would I be mad?

—Trust me. Men get mad. Especially when they say they have no reason to be mad.

—I'm not mad.

—It's not that I don't want you. I do, you know. I just have to clear my head a bit. So, a hug, okay?

We hugged on the bridge. She stood on her tiptoes to snake her arms around my neck, and for an electric split second, our mouths were dangerously close together. Instead, she held her cheek against mine.

I led her to her apartment building, above the Wilma Theater at the end of the bridge. We hugged at the door, and I again almost kissed her. Afterward, I walked home.

I was glad that my wife disapproved of dogs, otherwise its barking might have woken her up. Hungry, I sneaked into the kitchen. In the fridge, covered in tin foil and labeled with a post-it note bearing my name, was a dinner plate for me. I sat in the dark and ate.

5

I awoke early in the morning to the movement of my wife slipping out of our bed to perform her prayers. It was still dark. The only light was the ghostly green glow from the alarm clock. I did not need to look at the hour. It was three or four in the morning.

I heard her fumble around in the dark for her prayer mat. She unrolled it and lowered herself down. Her knees popped. In the quiet, it was like two gunshots in a cave. She paused, holding her breath, as if hoping she had not awakened me. I concentrated on making my breathing seem like that of a sleeping man. She began her morning prayer, mumbling the ancient words.

I am an atheist and have been since I was sixteen years old. It was not too long before I met my wife when I would have scoffed at a sight such as this. I based my self-esteem on my intelligence, on the fact that, as a non-believer, I was smarter than those that believed. As I have aged, my views have changed. Although my atheism has never wavered, I have come to respect private religion. This private religion, where one is alone, where one reflects on themselves and vows to become a better person. It is the public religion that turns ugly, the one that separates people by faith. The one that declares as enemies those that do not profess the same beliefs, even if the difference is slight.

There are some of my non-faith that believe the only way to create peace in this world is to wipe all trace of religion away. I do not think this is true. The will to control, the will to force others to your way of thinking is a human flaw, not a religious one. It rears its head when like-minded people form a cohesive group. If religion were banished, something else would fill the vacuum. As I lie in bed, an image runs through my brain of scientists and doctors wielding microscopes like clubs above their heads, rounding up citizens and forcing them to pledge allegiance to Carl Sagan or face death.

My wife finished her prayers, rolled up the mat and got ready for work in the dark. I told myself to get out of bed. I should start a conversation with her, no matter the topic—anything that might open the lines of communication that had been closed so long.

If I got up, however, she would have felt guilty for making too much noise. The next day she would get up earlier, so she could move even slower and make less noise. I decided that I would wait until she had left the room, after she had gone downstairs and begun making breakfast. I would act natural. I would say that I just woke up and wow did her cooking smell good.

My feigned sleep instead turned to real sleep and I did not open my eyes again until several hours later. When I went downstairs, my wife was gone.

An hour later, I was heading out to Frenchtown, the small town directly to the west. I was in a sour mood, not due to my hangover, but rather due to the person who was sharing my cab. His name was Trevor and I hated him. He was in his late twenties and had poor hygiene and even worse social skills. He had greasy brown hair and scabs on his cheeks that never seemed to heal. His ripped coat smelled of mildew and stale smoke. He picked his nose when he thought I wasn't looking. Unlike the rest of us in the company, Trevor did not drive his own truck. Instead he floated around from truck to truck, ostensibly to help roll out hoses and dig for the tanks, but in reality he only served to piss us off. Of course, I complained. Everyone complained about him, but he had some agreement with

Maureen that kept him employed, albeit just barely.

We pulled up to a group of new houses in a small development along the Frontage Road. In front of the house was a blond-haired girl who looked to be fourteen years old, balancing a baby in her thin arms. Only when I got out of the truck did I realize that she was older than I thought and was most likely the child's mother.

—Mrs. Davenport, correct? I asked.

The woman blinked her green eyes. The baby in her arms fidgeted.

—Yes?

—My name is Mr. James.

—It's nice to meet you James. You can call me Sarah.

—No. James is my last name. Bridger is my first name.

She looked confused, so I changed the subject.

—I hear we got a problem?

—I see, yes. Well, the problem's in back.

—We'll follow you.

Mrs. Davenport led us to the back of the house. The problem was immediately apparent. The ground was spongy and wet. The faint smell of feces wafted up whenever one of us took a step.

—Septic tank's backed up, Trevor said. —Sure as shit. Ha, ha. Pun intended.

He wiped his mouth and spat on the ground. I saw him eyeing the young mother. It was good that she was so distracted, because the look would have made her skin crawl.

—Trevor, why don't you go to the truck and get the hoses ready.

—Fuck you, he said, oblivious to good manners. —I'm not going to wait by the truck like some bitch.

I leaned my head over and whispered into his ear. His eyes widened.

—I'll get the hoses, he said.

He left.

Because it was a newer home, the septic tank had a riser to it, that is, an above-ground connection to the tank, so we wouldn't have to dig. Mrs. Davenport pointed out the riser hidden behind a lilac bush. I thanked her and told her she could wait inside. Trevor came with the hoses and hurried back to the truck to maintain his court-ordered distance from her child. I had no inclination to join him.

I had a hunch about why Mrs. Davenport had a problem. I knew what to look for, so I tried to find risers in the backyards of each of her three neighbors. I found none.

—Mr. Bridger? Mrs. Davenport said from behind me.

—Bridger, just Bridger, I said.

—I made some sandwiches. Not just now. I made them a little while ago. Earlier. For you.

—I'd be glad to, I said. —Thank you.

—I'll go get your friend. You can go inside. Make yourself at home. That's what people say.

—Don't bother. It's company policy that we can't have the truck unattended. People steal from the cab.

This was not company policy, but it would not be good to tell her the true reason Trevor had to stay away. It would give me some time away from him. As to people stealing from the cab: yes, that was true.

Mrs. Davenport's kitchen was bland and non-descript. It didn't look lived in yet. The walls were white and the linoleum was white save for a few pink flowers between the squares. Leaning against one wall was a framed reproduction of a painting, waiting to be hung. I excused myself and washed my hands in the bathroom.

When I came back to the kitchen, a plate stacked high with egg salad sandwiches lay on the table. Next to it was a pitcher filled with red Kool-Aid. Mrs. Davenport watched me as I bit into a sandwich, not eating any herself.

—It's good, I said, more out of politeness than truth.

—Thank you. I looked up the recipe on the Internet.

I'm not used to making things for people.

She sighed and turned her eyes to the wall. They were lovely eyes that I could tell would burn out too soon. I poured myself a glass of Kool-Aid.

—Is it true what your partner said? That the septic tank is full?

—It seems that way.

—How can that be? We just moved in this summer. I mean, we couldn't have . . . pooped that much.

—That's not the problem. Sometimes a lot of water gets in during the construction process. After this pump, you should be good for three to five years.

I didn't tell her what I suspected. That the lack of risers in her neighbors' yards meant all the surrounding houses drained into the same septic tank, the one for which she was responsible. The developers had probably done this to save money. If that was the case, the problem wasn't going to be fixed without a whole lot of money and an army of lawyers.

—I'm not one to complain, I said, —but I think there's something wrong with the Kool-Aid.

—What? she said, snapping out of her malaise.

—It doesn't have any sugar.

The red liquid was terribly bitter. I made an effort to swallow what was in my mouth.

—Oh god. I forgot to put it in!

Mrs. Davenport grabbed the pitcher and rushed to the sink. She had poured half of the Kool-Aid off before she stopped. She must have realized she could have fixed the problem by adding some sugar. She took a step back.

—It's okay. Please. Water is fine. I shouldn't be drinking something with so much sugar. Please, just a cup of water.

Mrs. Davenport poured me a glass of water. I ate in silence and she stared at the wall. It was not long before I could not stand it.

—You're not from around here, I said. —I can tell by your accent.

—Really? I thought I talk normal. No, I'm from Connecticut.

—Connecticut? I used to live in New York City for a couple of years.

For the first time, emotion graced her face. Her lips curled into a smile.

—Not the same thing.

Then it was gone.

—I miss the ocean.

—I do too, sometimes.

More silence.

—I have no friends here.

—Listen, things will change, I said. —You'll make friends. People are friendly out here. They may not seem that way. Sad to say, some think you're an outsider if you're not born here. Hell, there's some people that'll treat you that way unless you got five generations born here before you.

Another pause.

—Nobody told me it was going to be this hard.

I did not know what to say to that. I thought to give a standard response, that parenting is hard, that making friends is hard, you just need to stick to it, but the words had the bitter taste of inauthenticity on my tongue. Truly my own experience was more difficult than most, with the doctors and the anguish of having produced a broken child. These words instead tasted of pride, saying that the girl had no room to complain. Many words were tried in my brain. All were rejected.

From the living room came a cry from her baby. Mrs. Davenport, it was strange to call this person little older than a girl, didn't react. I ate another sandwich and finished my glass of water. Finally, Mrs. Davenport got up and went into the living room. I stayed still, wondering if it was too much of a breach of etiquette to just leave. Eventually she came back, holding the now calmed baby with its head resting against her shoulder.

—I don't understand it, she said. —Sometimes he'll cry for hours and nothing I do can make him stop. And other times, he's an angel.

I nodded.

—I'll get a few of these wrapped up for your friend. I don't want him to go–

Suddenly we heard a loud bang coming from the front of the house, followed by a stream of muffled curse words. I leapt out of the chair and stomped through the front of the house, leaving dirt marks on the snow-white carpet of the living room.

Outside, Trevor stood next to the truck, pounding the hose coupling with a hammer and trying to uncouple it with a wrench. From under the coupling came a thin trickle of sewage water.

—Trevor, I shouted, —what did you do?

—I didn't do fucking nothing.

I went over and pushed him out of the way. I struggled with the wrench to stop the leak. Trevor hopped around in anxiety.

—I can do it, fuckface. Don't fucking treat me like a child.

He tried to muscle his way in. I tried to shrug him off, but he pushed. I had almost gotten the leak stopped when he pushed with all he had.

It happened.

The coupling broke off the threads. A geyser of sewage water shot out of the pipe and drenched me, drenched Trevor, and drenched Mrs. Davenport's front yard.

I managed to stop the flow, but the truck was messed up. I couldn't get the leak to stop completely. A gasket was busted and I had no replacement. Explosions are not lenient to rubber. I told Trevor to spray down the driveway while I gathered up the main hose and tried to pretend we were never there. I talked to Mrs. Davenport through the sliding glass window, begging her not to open it. She didn't quite listen to what I said. She rocked the baby in her arms and stared out over my shoulder.

—I'm very sorry.

—I'm sorry, too, she said.

We drove away. This woman would have a hell of a time explaining what happened when her husband got home. Hopefully, he'd be of the right mind and call us up and leave abusive messages with our answering service rather than taking it out on her. We probably should have stayed longer, made sure we cleaned the driveway better, but no matter what we did, things would stink for a long time.

All the way back to Missoula, Trevor swore. He furiously spat on the floor and checked his teeth in the rearview mirror.

—Some of it got in my fucking mouth!

—Why was your mouth open?

—I didn't have my mouth open. It just got in there. This is serious. I could get AIDS from this, right? Tell me that I can't get AIDS.

—Actually, I'm pretty sure it's the only way people get AIDS.

—Fuck you man. That's not real.

—Oh, it's real.

That was the end of Trevor's profane tirade. I tried not to crack a smile as he sat there trying to decide whether to believe me or not.

When we pulled into headquarters, he immediately leapt out of the truck and headed inside, ignoring my warning against it. I parked the truck around the corner of the building to screen myself from any onlookers, attached the clean water hose to a spigot, and stripped down to my skivvies. My heart seized up and threatened to stop for good as I ducked under the freezing cold water. I hopped around for warmth and shouted.

A few minutes later, I heard yelling. From around the truck, Trevor stumbled backward while a red-faced

Laura pushed him.

—I'm just trying to take a shower, you bitch! Trevor yelled.

—What the hell are you doing tracking that shit into the main office? We got carpet. What's a customer going to think if we got a set of shitty footprints straight through the office?

—I can't walk around like this all day. What am I supposed to do?

—Do what Bridger's doing, she said.

I stood there spraying down my soiled pants and shirt and jacket with the hose. I smiled and waved cheerfully, although I was sure that I was turning blue.

—Hi sexy, Laura said with a smile before filling her face full of fury and glaring at Trevor again.

Trevor stood there. His mouth was full of rage, working up the devastating insults. His fists clenched up, and I was worried I would have to step in to keep him from attacking Laura, me in my skivvies and all. Then he burst out crying. He cried loudly and childishly. He brought his hands to his mouth to wipe away drool, only catching himself just before the flesh of his excrement-covered hands made contact. Instead, he held them at his chest and shook them.

—Am I going to get fired? he sobbed. —I need this

job, please. I can't work anywhere else. Please don't fire me.

—We won't … or at least I won't. Here, let Bridger help you clean up.

Trevor walked over to me, and I helped the sobbing man out of his soiled clothes. Laura smiled at us as she walked away.

—Have fun, boys, she said.

I cleaned him up as best I could and helped him back into his clothes. He had stopped crying, but was still very shaken up. I promised him a ride home, as there was no way he was in any shape to ride the bus. I had him sit in the car while I went up to the office and knocked on the door. Laura answered with her beautiful smile, which quickly turned into a frown.

—My mom wants you to go home, she said.

—I figured that, I said. —I already got the chosen one bundled up and ready for bed.

I pointed over my shoulder at my car. We laughed.

—Admit it, I continued. —You like that. You like feeling powerful.

—Honestly, I can't think of a job I'd like doing better than making grown men cry.

—You should be a drill sergeant. That's what they do all day.

—Ha. I don't think I would pass the physical, Laura said, thumping her chest.

We laughed some more, and then were quiet long enough for it to get awkward. I leaned in to hug her goodbye, but stopped just before. Laura had her hands up and her face wore mock horror. I smiled and nodded to my car.

6

When I got home, I took a hot shower. I still felt dirty, so I took a bath. I used my wife's special soaps but only ended up with skin that smelled like lilac-scented shit. I worried I would never lose that smell.

Frustrated and depressed, I bundled myself into a bathrobe and went to the upstairs den. Eppy played with her toys. Her back was turned and I slipped in unnoticed. My daughter babbled to herself in her private language. No real words were among them, but after so much silence from her, it was something. As she played, unaware of me, I brought my hands together in two heavy claps.

I was not alone among parents who didn't believe their child's diagnosis, or imagined that one day the deformed bones and twisted nerves would miraculously knit together, or that their child was just stubborn all along or that this was just a prank that had held up for years and years.

I was glad to see that Eppy still played with toys. But in a few years, she would reject her childhood and burn with impatience as she waited to grow up. She would reject all the things that gave her joy and instead focus on things that would cause her anguish: her looks, her popularity. Given her disability, no matter how beautiful a woman she blossomed into, she would always be an outsider.

She finally noticed me. She looked shocked, that animal fear of predators rising up to the surface. Then she giggled and walked over to me, dragging her knuckles along the ground as if she were a gorilla. Clutched in one hand was a faded and worn stuffed yellow duck that she had had since she was a toddler. She threw it in my lap.

Let's play a game, she signed.

—What sort of game?

She giggled again and gorilla-walked back to her pile of toys. She picked out another stuffed animal and dragged it over to me. She threw the stuffed dog in my lap next to the duck.

—I need to know what sort of game it is before I decide I want to play. What kind of game is it, Eppy?

A game game.

She continued to drag over stuffed animals until she ran out. Then she did her funny walk to the linen closet and brought out extra pillows and a quilt. From her room, she dragged out a few of her dresses. We laughed together. She stood before me, bent over with laughter at me in my blanket cocoon, when the door opened. In the doorframe was my wife. Her face registered confusion, and then a flash of anger. Her lips parted and she looked on the verge of saying something, but then shook her head and went into our bedroom. Eppy and I were silent for almost a minute after she left.

Mommy's very mad at us, she said.

There was something in the way she signed that made me feel that she was whispering.

—No, I don't think that is it, I whispered back. —There is something wrong, though. Eppy, put these away.

I indicated the blankets and stuffed animals. She pouted.

Help me put these away. You were playing, too.

—No, Eppy.

I helped my wife as she struggled to get out of her dress. Sitting on the edge of the bed in her slip, she rubbed the sides of her head. I sat down at the far edge of the bed, the furthest away I could be from her without falling off, and waited. I knew that I should say something, but I knew nothing that would ease her pain, at least through words.

—You need aspirin? I asked.

She said nothing. I knew that she did not take aspirin and refused to take anything but her blood pressure medication. It was a pain to get her to take that. My offer of aspirin was more to cut the silence than to do anything else.

—At least let me get you a glass of water.

I went downstairs without waiting for a response. I had to get out of there. While downstairs, I picked up an envelope and brought it with me.

Upstairs, my wife lay down on the bed. Her necklace and earrings were in her hands. I gave her the glass of water, which she sat up and sipped. I took her jewelry from her and put it in the box on her night table. Some, but not enough of the tension drained from her face. I handed her the letter, and the tension came back. She took the letter, barely glancing at the Arabic scrawl on the return address, and then leaned over to slip it inside the night table.

—You know you don't have to open that.

My wife made a movement that would be imperceptible to someone who had not been married to her for almost ten years: an infinitesimally slight nod. Then she tore the letter open and unfolded it. These letters from family members made her cry. This one was no exception.

My wife stopped talking about her family after her father died a little over a year after our marriage. It was as if the only person that she felt she needed to talk to me about, the one that represented her, was gone and the rest of her family was dead, even if a few of them didn't quite know it. According to her, the letters were only updates: who got married, who died. I once took a bit of Arabic, listening to CDs and reading a few books checked out from the library. By no means had I learned enough to speak the language, but I could pick out a few words. I think some of the letters asked for money, and I know at least one brother was furious that she lived in the West and had married a Westerner. Again, my command of the language never got beyond the most basic, and I might have misconstrued everything. I never had the head for foreign words.

My wife never listened to me when I pleaded with her to not read these letters. Although it frustrated me, I understood. For years, my mother called me on a near daily basis. In these phone calls she did two things: she complained and she wished. She complained about my grandmother's illness, the old house empty without my father, the midnight barking of the neighbor's dog. She wished that I would get a girlfriend, get a job, get a better job. I would listen distractedly while watching a TV show on mute and spooning ramen noodles into my mouth. For all the things we talked about, the true emotion behind these calls was never said. My mother was angry at me. I had left her alone. Even when my grandmother was alive, even when my father was still alive, she was alone. She was angry that I hadn't turned out the way she wanted, a copy of my dead older brother and the opposite of my father. She was angry that I had not given her enough time to chip off those bits of my character she did not like, those bits that I had learned to harden over time.

I stopped studying Arabic when my wife realized that I had been reading her letters. She did not confront me, but began keeping the letters under lock and key. I was too ashamed to continue with the lessons. I had violated her privacy, and she would never trust my intentions. The letters still came every few months. She still read them even though they made her cry.

I went into the bedroom and found a tissue. She dried her eyes and put the letters away in a small cabinet next to our bed, joining the voluminous stack of others. One thing had changed. She trusted me enough not to lock the cabinet.

I left and went into Eppy's bedroom. I helped her put everything away. By the time we were done, it was her bedtime, and after much cajoling, pleading and negotiating, I managed to get her ready for bed. I read her a bedtime story while lying on her bed, with her curled up in my arms. I knew that she could not hear me. When her eyes fluttered closed, she could no longer read my lips. Instead she held onto my hand while I stumbled through the words via sign language, trying to catch the last words as she drifted off to sleep. I slept there that night, with my daughter curled up in the crook of my arm.

7

I sat at the counter at the Oxford that Saturday eating a late lunch with Chet. I was finishing up a plate of JJ's while Chet complained of stomach problems. He crushed some pills between the back of a spoon and a couple of napkins, and stirred the powder into his milk.

—You keep eating that spicy stuff, you get my age, you're going to have problems, Chet said.

—I get your age, I'm killing myself. Nobody wants to be as old as you.

Chet raised the corner of his mouth, and gave a weak chortle. I felt guilty trying to keep up our game of insults when he didn't feel up to it. The thing was, I didn't know how to interact with him except via insults. I knew next to nothing about him. I knew his opinions on politics and religion, both of which he felt were a pile of shit. I knew that he had three sons. Two of them picked him up late at night. I got the feeling his third son and him didn't get along. The simple way to learn more, and probably the correct thing to do, was to ask him, "How are you doing, really?" He looked up at me, and I opened my mouth to ask him, when the portable radio on our table erupted in cheers. The local football team, the Montana Grizzlies, had scored. Any thought of opening up was gone from both our minds.

We listened to the game, talking stats and playoff chances. To be a man in America, you need to be able to at least bluff your way through American football. Perhaps we need this buffer between us, this wall of protection, a way to start a conversation. The human animal needs to act with its peers. We talk about football as men, because it is a way to open the conversation; otherwise we would not be able to talk at all. Once the silence is broken, they can then steer the conversation towards themselves. People are, at the core, jealous when it comes to emotions.

We all have these words trapped behind a barrier within us. That barrier strains against the weight of emotion. Perhaps it would be a beautiful world where, when asked how you are feeling, you could be fully honest and get those words out before they tear a hole in the side of your heart. I doubt, however, that a listener could last long against that torrent of raw feeling.

I came back to the present after Chet groaned in agony when the opposing team ran back the kick for a large gain. I shook my head, hoping that he hadn't noticed me zoning out, then agreed with him that the refs were giving the game to the other team.

The bells on the door jingled as it opened. In came a blonde woman with heavy makeup, thin arms and wide hips. She wore a small white T-shirt that exposed the wrinkly fat on her belly. Her thighs threatened to burst her too-tight jeans. She wore a smile that hinted that her mind and perhaps her sanity were miles away. The thick foundation of her makeup did not quite cover the bags under her eyes.

She went to the last stool at the restaurant counter and sat facing away from Mick, as if pretending she had not noticed him. When Mick saw her, he scowled a scowl that carved wrinkles as deep as canyons on his face. He stalled for time by wiping down glasses for customers that weren't there.

Finally, he walked to the woman and put a hand on her shoulder. She turned to him and smiled. Mick did not smile back, only asking what she wanted in a gruff tone. I did not hear the rest of the conversation, but I heard him becoming more and more frustrated. After a few minutes of this, the tension crackling in the air, he reached into his pocket and pulled a few bills from his wallet. She rose, gave him a kiss on his cheek, and left the bar. He went back to wiping glasses. I could see the bitterness build on his face, the words trapped behind the barrier. He walked over to us.

—How's the niece? Chet asked.

—God, crazy as always. Needed some money to go to a music festival. She said she only needed a little food money. Said she was going to hitchhike there, stupid dumb . . .

He trailed off, not allowing himself to call her what he wanted to call her.

—Some people it seems just want people to give up on them, Chet said.

—I should have given up a long time ago, Mick snorted. —You coming over for a drink?

I tipped over my watch arm to check the time.

—It's three o'clock, Mick, I said.

—It's about six hours too early to start drinking, Chet said.

—Well, I opened up at eight, so the way I see it, you're seven hours too late. What? You got somewhere else to be?

Chet and I looked at each other. Neither one of us had a good excuse to refute what Mick said. I got up and rolled Chet's wheelchair over to the bar.

I was good and drunk by seven o'clock. I felt self-conscious. Most everyone else was just starting their night, and here I was struggling to get my legs to remember how to stand up straight. Chet, of course, had switched over to straight diet coke hours ago. He waited for his sons to come pick him up. They arrived about 8:30 in a gray panel van. White putty filled in the moonscape of dents. Chet wheeled himself out to the van and I followed. Two of his sons, both in their early twenties, wore their black hair tied up behind their heads. One of the sons, Tommy I think it was, had an arrowhead dangling from an earring and a necklace of seashells around his neck. The other, who by elimination had to be Shawn, wore a neon pink shirt advertising a cancer fundraiser over a decade in the past, sunglasses that hung on a rainbow-colored thong, and flip-flops. In my drunken state, I mused that he must have been sporting the native garb of the Neo-Uber-Techno tribe before I realized that that was a very racist thing to think and I hated myself for it.

—Did you really mean it, I asked, —when you said that some people want to have their loved ones give up on them?

—What?

—Earlier today, when Mick's niece came in.

—Hold on, Tommy, stop the lift. Sure, sure. There's people who want others to give up on them. They like to see just how far others will go to help them. It's like they can't feel love properly. They push it as far as they can. The worse it gets, the more humiliation others are willing to suffer for them, the more they feel loved.

I realized that I had gotten his two sons mixed up again. Tommy was the one in the neon shirt.

—Is somebody trying to get you to give up on them?

—No, I said.

—You trying to get somebody to give up on you?

I hesitated and that was all the answer he needed.

—Your wife?

—She deserves better, I said, a little too loudly.

Saying that cut through me deep. If I hadn't been so drunk I would have been too ashamed.

—Listen, you ain't so bad. Lot of other women out there have husbands that beat them and put cigarettes out on their skin. You got a stable job, if not a well-paying one. She don't have to worry about begging on the street, and I've seen how well you treat your daughter. A woman needs that in a man.

I tried to thank him, but the words got stuck. The edges of my tear ducts burned.

—But just because you ain't so bad doesn't mean you ain't so good either. You're still a pile of shit. You just don't stink as bad as the rest of them.

He nodded over at Tommy, who restarted the lift. I was happy to be back on insulting terms. Although it was necessary to sometimes bare open your chest to another human being, it was painful. The nerves were raw and ragged, and someone could really fuck you up if you let them in there too long.

—So don't get yourself a big head, Chet said.

—See you soon, you giant sack of shit? I asked.

—See you.

I waved as Chet's sons got in and started the engine. As the panel van pulled away, through the window, Chet flipped me off with a smile.

I stood on the street corner for several more moments, letting that sink in. I went back inside to collect my coat. Before I could grab it, Mick put a fresh beer down in front of me.

—This one's on me, he said.

I sighed. Mick never bought me a beer unless he knew I was about to leave. It was his trick to keep people in the bar, keep them paying more money. I sat down and drank the beer. Then I drank four more before I stumbled my way home.

8

I awoke the next morning to an empty bed and a dull throbbing way back in my skull. Throughout the day the throbbing would get worse unless I took some aspirin, but it was nice not feeling like I'd been hit in the forehead with a shovel first thing in the morning.

I wandered over to Eppy's room and then downstairs before I realized my wife and daughter were gone. For a moment, my scrambled brains told me that it had happened, my wife had packed both their suitcases and left me. No, my wife's things were there. Eppy wouldn't have left without her favorite toy, a silver scooter on which she raced through the streets and terrified her father.

I decided to go for a walk. The fresh air would be good. I went upstairs and dressed. But no matter where

I looked, I could not find my wallet. I had lost it twice since returning to Missoula, and I did not look forward to having to gather all those documents again. I searched through my bedroom, first checking my pants, which, although dirty, my wife had folded and placed on a chair. I checked the night table and under the covers. With my hangover and dismay growing, my search went downhill. I spent most of the time pacing back and forth, muttering under my breath that it had to be fucking somewhere, before I found it in the third drawer of our oak dresser. I tried to connect the dots in my head as to why I had put it there rather than somewhere I could get to easily, but I doubted my mind had been even capable of making memories the night before.

When I pulled out the wallet, I noticed something shiny below it: two keys on a ring and a decorative fob. I stared at them for a moment, trying to remember what they unlocked. I dug around the drawer again, finding more sets of keys. It was then that I remembered my wife's habit of never throwing keys away. I was never sure why she did that. Certainly, the locks would have been changed on all those homes and apartments, and my wife had no intention of returning. I grabbed the keys on the fob, and sat on the edge of the bed.

One key was silver and the other bronze. The fob was circular, maybe two to three inches wide and an eighth of an inch thick and made of brass. Cut out of the center, a monkey walked on all fours, its tail in the air. It was something one would find in a tourist kiosk or museum gift shop. It was then that my memory jolted forward to tell me it was from the gift shop of the art museum where my wife worked. These were the keys to her apartment when we met. I remember making a stupid joke about these being her "mon-keys." I was lying on her bed while she removed her makeup in the vanity mirror. I remember her looking back at me without expression. That was the first day she had invited me to her place, and I thought for sure she would break up with me after that joke.

She could only afford a small studio, even with the healthy paycheck from the museum. The place was dim and oppressive, with little natural light, but one window showed a sliver of the ocean. She had placed a floral print armchair in front of it, and sat there reading books, every so often looking up and staring at that deep patch of blue.

Those were the happy days of our relationship. They weren't the only happy days. The days between the time

Eppy was born and the stressful days after we found out she was deaf were good days. Back then, we lived in a peaceful silence. I remember feeling happy that I had found someone with whom I could feel comfortable *not* talking. Someone I could sit beside without feeling the need to pollute the air with words. Back then my wife's and my relationship was strong—she spent our time together reading, and I spent the time coming up with jokes that, if not exactly sparking laughter, at least made her lift one corner of her mouth into a smile.

The courtship was short and without any true feeling. We had not had time to disbelieve the shadow play. All lovers create an image of their beloved in their minds. This image is pure and perfect and completely divorced from reality. Truth is, people are people and people are imperfect. If she had spent more time with me, if we had had a longer engagement, she would have never married me. I remember waking up the first night after our wedding, looking over at the fine black hairs growing out of her lower back, and realizing that I had a real person in my bed, and that real person was as flawed as I was. No, that is not true. My wife was as close to that faultless image as any person could come. I was a mess.

For what reason my wife held onto her old keys, I

did not know. Perhaps they were a connection to her past, a statement that those pathways were to remain open. If she were to throw the keys away, she would be cutting off those memories, keeping them locked forever out of her mind and out of her heart.

As I sat on the edge of the bed, fingering her "mon-keys," I wondered if she would keep the keys to this house when she finally left. This would be one burden that she would not wish to carry with her. This would be one memory, the door to which she should permanently close. It would depend on how things ended. I would gladly give her the house, but as she would not wish to stay in Missoula, it would be of no use to her. She might be able to sell it, although from what I had heard, with the housing market so depressed, that process would take a long time. I could see her going from room to room, packing each box with care, ensuring that the only things that she'd take with her had no connection to me. She would come across this dresser and wonder why she still had the keys to her studio apartment. Were they worth the box space? Would the good memories she had of that apartment, of reading in her armchair and staring at her tiny patch of water, be enough to remove my corruption? I hoped they would.

I heard the downstairs door open, the heavy patter of feet and Eppy's bubbling laughter. Downstairs my wife put away the groceries while Eppy jumped back and forth like a skier in a slalom race. I joined in and then we set the table. My wife cooked eggs and potatoes while Eppy and I folded the white cloth napkins into sailor's hats. It was a good day.

9

—Bridger, I need you if you have a minute, Maureen called from her office.

I had half a mind to walk out the door, pretending I had not heard. I guessed what she wanted and for what she might be asking. She had asked me this favor before. But if I wanted to get on the Winter List, I needed to be the one on whom she depended.

—Maureen, I said as I squeezed into her office.

—Trevor didn't come in yesterday, you know. He didn't come in today.

—So?

—I need you to go by his house, knock on the door.

—Did you call him?

Maureen gave me an acid glare.

—Of course you called him, I said.

—Just a quick knock on the door. If he doesn't

answer, don't bother.

—You could just fire him, I said, pushing my luck.

Again with an acid glare, stripping off two layers of my skin. A look that said she didn't like being told how to run her business.

—I'll swing by, I said.

—Good. If he's there, take him on the job with you. I'll deal with putting him on the clock. Just call me.

As I got into my truck and pulled out of headquarters, I thought about what she was asking me to do. I was not going there to tell him to come to work; I was to make sure he hadn't killed himself. Given his restrictions, it wasn't far-fetched for him to do it. As morbid as it sounded, I sometimes wondered why he hadn't. Of course, suicide is wrong, but in some situations, it is hard to explain why that is. If Trevor had a wife and kids, yes, it would be wrong. But he had no wife and no kids. He once told me, when he showed up to work drunk and I had to drive him home, that he hadn't had a girlfriend since middle school. If he had parents to mourn him, it would be wrong, but they were long gone. If he even had friends . . . I knew that if Maureen were to one day tell the crew that he had offed himself, we would all say that it was sad, but would think that at least we'd never have to go on a job with him again.

I pulled up at Trevor's place about thirty minutes later. It was in a duplex at the end of a cul-de-sac. Pieces of white Styrofoam fluttered in the wind above the brown, patchy grass.

From the window facing the street came the drone of guitars from a heavy metal song. A Confederate flag hung in the window, even though I knew that Trevor didn't come from the South. I knocked on the door twice. There was no answer. Through the window, I saw Trevor sitting on the floor playing a video game. He wore bulky headphones over his ears. The logic behind his blaring music while listening to something else on headphones was not something I could understand.

I had done my duty. I had proof that he was not dead, so I might as well have gotten on with my day. But Maureen had told me to take him along if I could. I knocked again, knowing that he could not hear me. I tried the door, thinking that if it were locked, I could say that I tried but I couldn't get his attention. In an act of supreme betrayal, the door opened without resistance. I walked inside. Trevor must have seen my reflection in the television because he jumped in fright.

He turned and shouted at me. I shouted back. With

a remote, he turned the thrumming guitars down.

—Fuck me! Don't sneak up on me like that, he shouted. —You know I could have shot you. That'd be within my rights! Anybody who comes in my home, I can legally shoot!

—You're not allowed to have a gun.

I did not know if that was true. From the frustration on Trevor's face and his silence, I guessed that it might be true.

—Come on, Trevor, I said. —It's time to go to work.

He glared at me for a few moments. Then he spun around and unpaused his game.

—I'm not going back. Fuck that place.

The voice in the back of my head again told me that I had done my duty. Maureen would not be angry with me if I left after he flatly refused.

I stood there over him, ticking through the several arguments I could use. What are you going to do about money? How are you going to pay rent? All these questions that form the bars of our carefully crafted prisons when all we want to do is live natural. Perhaps the most noble way to live is face down in a ditch. Yet, this dream of freedom means nothing without the prison. To be human is to deny one's desires, to shake the bars of our cage in fury, when in truth they are only made of paper. The dog does not deny itself, it does not feel guilt for its happiness. A survival mechanism? Did human existence only evolve this way because we chose to store our nuts instead of eating them right away?

In the end, I did not need to convince Trevor of any checked questions about the need for survival.

—You want to sit down? Sure could use your help with these alien sons of bitches. You play? Don't worry, just don't suck.

—I can't. I gotta go.

—Don't leave! he said, in a voice more desperate than he'd probably intended. —Come on, man.

Trevor and I stared at each other, each realizing that we had almost had a moment.

—We're friends, aren't we? he asked. —I mean, not good friends, but still friends.

—Yes, we're friends, I said, although it felt like I was betraying a kingdom to an assassin.

He put down his game controller and stood up. The game continued without him. His avatar was shot several times and crumpled to the ground.

—You know any girls? No, why would you know girls? You're married. But I was reading that dating websites suck and the only way to meet girls is through friends. I wish I had friends, you know, but everyone's so fucking hollow. Like they all got this shovel and they dig out everything that's interesting so there's only shit left. I don't want fucking none of that. I want to be me. I want to act as crazy as I want because it's fun, okay? You fucking understand that? And don't you goddamn tell me that I need to be myself. That's only true if you're one of those people. That's only valid if you got an acceptable kind of weird. But if you're weird like me, forget about it. I got problems. I know that. If that bitch hadn't have told her mother about us. If her mother hadn't forced her to say that we fucked and gotten the cops on my ass, maybe I'd have less problems, but I'd still have problems. Just it'd be easier to live without everyone who knows about it thinks I'm after their kids, but . . . you know. We can't change some shit.

I understood him. I did not say so, but I did. I did not question further about this girl and their relationship. I asked if he'd like to come with me. He said no. I gave him a hesitant pat on the arm, for which he called me faggot, but it was a friendly insult. I shivered at the thought of calling him my friend, but that was that. Trevor sat down in front of his TV, turned the heavy metal up full blast, and snapped the headphones over his head.

After leaving Trevor's place, I drove to my first of

two jobs. A forty-year-old woman answered the door in a faded pink bathrobe. Her too-thick makeup and the spacey way she talked bespoke mental illness. I hurried up that job and left as soon as I could. Then I drove up Pattee Canyon, along winding roads that wended their way through the nicer homes of Missoula until the homes eventually gave way to forest. Deep in that forest, I pulled into the driveway of an unfinished cabin. Black tarpaper, tacked in place with rounded planks of wood. Hearing my truck, about ten or so dogs leapt in defense of their home, circling my truck and barking. I had to drive slow to avoid running any of them over.

A thin man with a bushy yellow-gray beard met me on the front porch. We exchanged a greeting and names, and he led me to a field ringed by a wooden fence. He outlined the general location of the septic tank with his finger and returned to the cabin. It began to snow lightly. I collected my tools and starting digging out the septic tank lid. A few minutes later, just as I was ready to start pumping, he came back and handed me a drink in a mason jar. I was thirsty, and took a big swig before I knew what it was. The brown liquid turned out to be iced tea mixed with whiskey. My throat closed up and I almost gagged.

—I shouldn't be drinking. I'm working, I said.

The bushy bearded man leaned against a rickety wooden fence. He looked at me from the corner of his eye. I wondered if this job would be full of insanity like the last one.

—It's good though, I said.

I put the mason jar of booze on a rock and continued working.

—It's snowing, he said.

I already knew that, but looked around as if discovering it for the first time.

—Yes, it is, I said.

—Used to be we got our first big snow in October. That'd melt off in a day or two, then by now we'd have three, four feet of snowpack straight through the winter. Until March came.

—I hadn't noticed, I said. —I just moved back to Montana. I grew up here, though. I remember how much it snowed.

—Where'd you live before?

—Washington State, I lied.

He seemed the type to feel that people from elsewhere were ruining the state. He disliked me enough as it was, and I didn't want to make it worse.

—On the coast, it just rains a lot in the winter, I

said. —So, I don't know.

—We need the snow, he continued. —We don't have snow, we have a bad fire season. I know it don't matter to you folks down in town, but up in the canyon, we could lose everything.

—Yeah, that would be bad, I said, feeling that I had to say something and hoping that that would suffice.

—I don't like it. I don't like change. I moved up here from L.A. back in the eighties because of it. Now it's not freeways going in or skyscrapers going up, hell it's Mother Nature that's changing. I'm tired of change. My whole life has been one of change. Everybody's is. That's why we buy land and build houses. We think one day we'll outrun the change. It's no use. We always lose out in the end.

I could not think of anything to say to that. There was silence between us for some time.

—I got sausages cooking in the house. You want one, you come inside. No need to knock.

He went back into the cabin. I finished up my work as quick as I could, digging up the hatch, breaking up the sludge on the bottom of the tank with a stirring rod and attaching the hoses. After that, there was little to do but wait. The pump on the truck terrified the dogs, but the quivering hose fascinated them. They ran around barking at it. One leapt over the rock on which I had put the iced tea, knocking over the jar.

After I was done, I considered putting the empty jar on the front porch and leaving. I was not sure if that invitation to come inside was, in fact, an invitation. The bearded man didn't seem to care one way or the other. In the end, I knocked on the screen door.

—I told you there's no need to knock, came a voice from deep within the house.

Given the unfinished exterior of the house, I expected the interior to be the same. Instead, after a small entryway, I found a well-apportioned living room. A sofa and two overstuffed armchairs sat around a polished coffee table. The window curtains were made from patchwork quilts to hold out the chill of winter. Two bookshelves heavy with books stood along the walls. A small flat-screen TV sat in one corner.

—I see you don't mind too well, the bearded man said. —I told you not to knock. It's just as well. I wouldn't be here to tell you to take your shoes off and you'd track mud in everywhere.

I took off my shoes and slipped them next to his waiting boots. He came over and took the jar out of my hand.

—One of your dogs knocked it over.

—Which one, the crazy one with the stubby legs?

—I don't remember, I said.

—You want another?

—If I can get one without booze, that'd be great.

He gestured for me to sit down and then brought me a jar of iced tea. He made a fuss about setting up a TV tray for the meal. The house smelled like cooked meat, and when he brought it out, I was hungry. It came out on a large plate, two blackened sausages, runny beans, and a slice of white bread with butter. Some thought had been given to health as there was also a small salad smothered in Thousand Island dressing. The sausages tasted gamey and wild.

—Is this venison? I asked.

The man nodded. He picked at his own plate of sausages.

—Did you hunt the deer yourself?

—Yup. Over in Dillon area a few weeks ago. Have a buddy who owns a butcher shop. He cut it up and stuffed the sausages for me. You hunt?

—I haven't hunted in a long time. I went often as a kid, but I haven't since I got back.

We swapped hunting stories. The bearded man did most of the talking. I hadn't been hunting since I was fourteen years old. I couldn't recall much except how bored I was the whole time.

—Do you ever get lonely up here? I asked.

The abrupt change in topic startled him. The question hung heavy in the room.

—Aw hell, he said. —Of course, I get lonely up here, but I got my dogs.

—I don't mean that. I mean a woman or . . .

I cut myself off, realizing that it was the wrong thing to say. The bearded man's face cracked with anger.

—I don't think I know you enough to talk to you about that. And I don't think you should be asking such questions.

There was another heavy pause. I ran through several apologies in my head but came up empty. Finally, the bearded man spoke again.

—I guess you're right. You weren't talking about sex. I know it's different between dogs and people. I think that my dogs love me, and I'm sure they do in their dumb little minds. But their love is temporary. They love anyone who's willing to feed them. I stop feeding them, say I die or something, and some stranger down the road gives them food and takes them in, that stranger's got all their love now.

—No, he continued. —A love from a person is different, because they got rational thought in their skulls and they can see what a no-good pile of junk we are and they still decide to love us anyways. For we are all born broken and not a single one among us is truly deserving of love. That's what makes love so special, I guess. Because it is a gift. To love someone is to give them a gift they don't deserve.

The bearded man cut a sausage with his fork and popped it in his mouth. He chewed slowly, ruminating over words that must have been repressed for a long time.

—Once I finish up the house, he continued, —then I'll set about getting a wife. There's some good ones still out there. Maybe I'll drive over to Spokane on the weekends. There's more women out there, I suppose. I feel that maybe that's the reason work on the house has gone so slow. Not ready to get back out there.

We talked little after that. I finished my meal. He took my plate from me and we said goodbye. As I drove away, he watched me from the front porch and cursed out his stupid dogs for running in front of my truck. I managed to weave my truck out of the driveway and headed back to the shop.

By the time I got back, the shop was closed. I didn't realize how long I had stayed at the bearded man's. I went inside, filled out my timesheet and showered and changed my clothes in the small locker room. When I opened up my locker, a small white piece of paper fluttered out. It was a note from Laura, saying that if I had time, I should meet her at a restaurant at 7 p.m. I looked down at my watch to check the time. If I hurried, and the traffic was good, I could make it. I hopped in my sedan and drove to the restaurant. It started snowing harder.

Traffic was light and I made it there with time to spare. However, Laura was nowhere to be found. I didn't have my cellphone on me, and even then, Laura and I never exchanged texts as she didn't want my wife to find out about us. I sat on a bench just inside the front door and waited and waited. The girl behind the counter, a young girl in her twenties with black hair and a nose ring through her septum, came over to the bench several times and asked if I wanted anything. I told her that I was waiting for someone, each time with greater irritation. After forty-five minutes, I gave up and walked home in a huff.

While walking home, I saw Laura's familiar jacket and hood in the distance. I wanted so much to cross the street, to walk by her and get her completely out of my life. It would be hard to do because she was a coworker and the daughter of my boss. I could manage. I could be unemployed again. I could move out of my house, out of town and live as an alcoholic bum under a bridge. At that moment, anything could be more agreeable than to pretend that her not being there did not piss me off.

Laura stopped. She waved at me and I knew I could not hate her. She did not say hello or that she was sorry. Instead, her face expressed everything. She took my hand as the snow whirled around us and rubbed warmth into my fingers. Then she led me back to her apartment.

10

Hunnngh!

Laura lay on the floor of her apartment with her knees up in the air. She wore a faded gray and pink undershirt a few sizes too big. She beat her fists softly against her chest, knocking out the thick mucus built up on the side of her lungs. She exhaled sharply. The bubbling mucus in her lungs sounded like a piece of candy being unwrapped.

Hunnngh!

—I'm sorry, she said. —I know this is gross. I just got to finish these exercises. I've been ignoring them lately, that's why I had that attack today.

—I didn't know, I said.

—Because I didn't tell you, she said with a grin.

I sat on a high stool staring down at her. I tried to find a comfortable position for my legs, but could not.

Next to me was a round dinner table covered in a month's worth of unopened junk mail. A mishmash of unmatched furniture filled her apartment. Knickknacks smothered every horizontal surface with no rhyme or category. Posters of famous works of art adorned the white walls, affixed there by masking tape. It felt temporary, like everything would be put in its proper place one day if she only had the time. Or she must have been avoiding putting everything in order given how temporary the situation was.

She stood up and went to the bathroom. She coughed again and spit mucus into the sink. She came back out and lay stomach-side down on the floor. She lifted up the back of her shirt.

—I'm going to need your help here buddy.

I straddled her back and gently struck her with the heel of my hand over and over, taking her through the crud-cleaning exercises so that she could breathe normally.

Hunnngh!

—I'm sorry. I promise, I get done, I'm all yours.

I said nothing.

—They wanted me to stay over at the hospital for observation, but I couldn't break my promise to you. Besides, I try to stay away from that place as much as possible. Everyone's so down. How are you expected to heal if everyone's all down? All that negative energy, you know.

After I finished tapping, she stood up and went to her kitchen sink, spit up the phlegm, and turned on the faucet to wash it down.

—You want a glass of wine?

—I've been drinking too much lately, I said.

—Pfah! You're worrying over nothing.

I heard something soft hit the floor. Laura poured out two glasses and then walked out from around the counter. She was naked from the waist down.

—I've got to warn you, she said. —Drinking red wine makes my panties fall off.

—What does white wine do? Make you put them on your head?

She laughed, handed me the wine glass and then tried to sit on my lap. On the stool, it was impossible to find a position that was not awkward. She supported herself with one leg, then reached back and stroked my hair. We both stared out into space and drank our wine.

—In case you're one of those guys that waits for the girl to make the first move, Laura said, finally breaking the silence. —Me coming out without my panties. That's the first move.

Laura coughed and turned to me with a weak smile.

—Oh honey, what's wrong?

I looked away, unable to answer her question. I was no longer angry at her leaving me at the restaurant. She had a good excuse. It wasn't my wife. I still loved my wife but it had never been a sexual love. I needed a connection that my wife could not provide. Perhaps I was ashamed of needing someone, needing someone to breathe hot breath in my ear, needing someone to touch me and to sigh when I touched her.

—Is it me?

This triggered a short bout of coughing which she tried to suppress the best she could.

—No, it's not that.

—Your wife? You said you no longer talk together. Sometimes, when a woman gets to that age, she just doesn't want it, but I do and I'm here and I want you. And you at least got another four years with me. Don't you want me?

—I do.

—Then take me.

She rubbed her hips against mine. She turned and pressed her lips to the corner of my mouth. I resisted kissing her back. I closed my eyes in shame. Laura scooted her hips back and dragged her hands against my crotch. Even with a beautiful woman rubbing herself against my lap, I was not erect.

—Get hard for me, Bridger, she moaned.

I could hear the rasp of her disease in her lungs. She turned her head away and coughed. She closed her eyes until the attack passed, and then returned to rubbing herself against me. She arched her back and brought up my hands to cup around her breasts. She moaned as I touched her nipples with my thumbs. She unzipped my pants and dug around for my flaccid penis.

—Please, baby. Get hard for me. Get—

Laura's mouth erupted with furious coughing. She covered it, but not fast enough to avoid spraying my face with mucus. She raced into the bathroom. She coughed so hard I was afraid her entire lung would pop out. After the phlegm came the vomit. Her body, racked with spasms, could no longer control her basic functions. I gathered up her clothes and went into the bathroom, despite her protestations to stay out. I stayed with her and stroked her back until the attack stopped.

—Do I need to call a doctor?

She shook her head. I helped her to bed and into her underwear. I poured out her wine in the sink and poured a glass of water for her. Then I started up the nebulizer on her night table. It hummed and soon fog rolled out of the mouthpiece.

—I feel better, she said after several deep breaths of the medicine. —This helps a lot.

Her voice was still hoarse. She didn't look better; if anything she looked weaker. She motioned with her hand and made room for me on the bed next to her. I crawled in and threw the blanket over my legs. I squeezed her tight and held my ear against her back, listening to the roiling tempest in her lungs.

—When I went to high school there was a girl in the grade lower. She had the same thing as me. She died when I was seventeen, and I thought for sure I was next. But as a year went by, as three years went by, and I didn't get worse, I began to believe nothing would happen.

She finished her treatment and turned off the nebulizer. With the hum gone, I could hear the sounds of the night coming through the window: the sound of revelers and the distant whine of a siren.

—I really don't have a lot to be worried about. Life expectancy is thirty-eight, so I got another four years. Besides, every day doctors are coming up with new treatments. I won't be surprised if I outlive you!

She was in a better mood. I worried that she might try to make love with me again, but it seemed the attack had ended all thought of sex. Laura turned, pulled the covers over both of us and tucked her head into my chest. She breathed slowly, only occasionally stopping for a cough.

—Tell me about your wife, she asked when the silence had gone on too long.

—There isn't much to say.

—Well, I want to hear it. It'll help me get to sleep. Where did you meet?

—At a fundraiser for the museum she worked at. I wasn't planning on going, but my roommate had an extra ticket, so . . . . Anyways, there was a lot of booze there, but her and I were the only ones not drinking. I didn't drink back then.

—That's it? One of life's little accidents?

—That's it. I asked her on a date before I even knew that I was asking. She said yes. I spent the next week expecting her to cancel, but she didn't. Our first date was not a disaster, so we had another one. We got married in order not to be alone. We had a kid because that's what married people do.

—Thank you, she said.

—For what?

—For reminding mc that I am not the only one in this world that has problems.

She coughed again.

—Are you sure you don't want me to call the doctor?

Laura shook her head until the coughing subsided.

—This is normal. I always cough a lot before bed. No, the nebulizer helps a lot. I had an attack earlier today, and I could barely breathe. This is nothing like that. I'm fine. You can go if you want.

—I don't think I should.

—Yes, you should. You need to be home with your wife. She needs you and your daughter needs you, too. Just don't go right yet, okay? Hold me for a while. I've been humbled, and I want someone around so that I don't feel like a total waste of a human being.

I stayed with her until she fell asleep. She was breathing, if a bit too shallow, her sleep only occasionally interrupted by coughs. As I stroked her hair, I thought about her and her illness. I tried to step into her skin and experience the horror and terror she must have felt, but couldn't. The cause of cystic fibrosis was frighteningly simple. Her cells could not properly pass two chemicals across cell walls. Of the myriad of problems that resulted, the worst was the drying up of the mucus tasked to remove bacteria and foreign objects from the lungs. The chemicals her body could not handle, the ones that crippled her lungs, that allowed infections to rip apart the tissue until she could no longer draw breath, were salt and baking soda.

Two hours went by. I slipped out of bed as cautiously as I could. I bent down and kissed her on the lips.

I made it home at about four o'clock in the morning. I changed out of my clothes in the darkness. I washed in the bathroom, trying to get rid of any perfume Laura's embrace might have left behind. I slipped into bed next to my wife. I was hoping not to wake her, but she rolled over and held me, murmuring soft words. We made love for the first time in over a year.

11

Thursday afternoon, I found a note waiting for me at the office. Eppy was in trouble. She had hit a student again, and my wife needed me to pick her up. That night the museum was hosting a major fundraiser and my wife was too busy planning. I had no more jobs scheduled for that day, and there was no point in waiting around for another one. Winter had set in. That freezes up the jobs, quite literally. I told Maureen that I had to pick up my daughter and talk to the teacher about her behavior. Maureen waved me off and went back to her phone call.

It is strange going to a school in the middle of the day while classes are going on. My early memories of school were of motion and of chaos—kids shoving each other; boys pulling the hair of girls they liked and girls scolding the boys they did not like; teachers, with their monstrous presence, trying to shape order out of it all. This was all behind closed doors now, and the halls were empty.

In the distance, I saw a boy leaning over a water fountain. I recognized the boy. His name was Darrin, and he was Eppy's special needs classmate and her one true nemesis. He stood up straight, looked at me, and smiled a strange, lifeless smile. Darrin was tall for his age, almost five-foot five. His black hair was cropped close to his head. He clenched and unclenched his fists as if he were deciding whether to attack me. Something in his blue eyes made me feel I would lose if he did.

—Go back to class, Darrin, I said.

Darrin did not move.

—Aren't you supposed to be somewhere? I asked.

He rocked back and forth on his heels. His stare did not waver.

—Go back to class.

Then, without a word, the boy spun around and walked down the hall. I breathed a sigh of relief when he turned the corner.

No one was behind the front desk. I heard an electronic bell chime somewhere in the back of the main office. Soon, a happy-faced woman with several chins kicked off the floor with her feet and glided behind the front desk on a rolling chair. I gave her my name and told her I had an appointment with Miss Black.

Miss Black's office was not an office, but one among several cubicles jammed together in a space that was once a classroom. One rectangular section of the wall was brighter than the rest: the ghost of a blackboard. The cubicles were subdivided again, with three teachers sharing a space meant for one. I found Miss Black in one of the furthest cubicles. She didn't notice me. She had long black hair and wore a sea-green sweater and a necklace made up of flat bronze disks. My memory piped up to say she was the spitting image of one of my old teachers. I allowed myself to imagine that all teachers wore the same clothes, handing down their old ones when they retired. When I laughed at this, Miss Black quickly closed the computer window to a social media site and switched to the school homepage.

—Miss Black?

She said nothing, and then glanced at her open agenda book for my name.

—Mr. James.

—Bridger.

—I do want to keep this formal, Mr. James, so—

—Wait, I'm sorry. I'm so used to people getting my name wrong that I get confused when they get it right.

She stared unblinking.

—It's good to see you again, I said. —We met on the first day of school when Eppy enrolled. I'm not sure you remember that. I'm sorry I haven't been to any of the other meetings.

—I do remember you. It is good to see you. Thank you for coming down here. I'm sure you know, Eponine's in a bit of trouble. No, that is not the truth. She's in a lot of trouble.

—What did Darrin do now? I said, trying to bring in a little humor.

—Not Darrin. It was Simon Westbrook. Do you know who I'm . . . about whom I'm speaking?

I did not know who she was speaking about. To break the atmosphere, I tried humor again.

—If my little girl keeps this up, I might just have to sign her up for MMA fighting.

— . . .

—I'm sorry, I said.

—Violence in my class is not tolerated. Studies have shown that if a teacher or a parent does not take violence seriously, even if no one is seriously hurt, it will only lead to worse behavior in the future.

Miss Black stared at me with the most contempt her young face could muster. She adjusted her necklace in fury. I could not bring myself to be as somber as her, but I tried my best.

—Will she get suspended from school? I asked.

—No. Studies have shown that it is not exactly conducive to discipline to give troubled kids free days off.

—Suspensions aren't as bad as they used to be when mothers stayed home. I got suspended once. Mother glared at me all day. It was horrifying.

As I said that, I told myself she didn't need the excuse of a suspension to glare at me.

—I know that we haven't met since the first day of school. But I want you to know that I take my job very seriously. I may be young, but I read a lot.

—I understand that. I *do* care about my daughter. I've been trying to get a meeting with you for a few weeks now.

—About taking Eponine out of the Special Needs class.

—And? I said after a pause.

—Completely out of the question.

—Why not? I mean, Eppy's a bright girl, brighter than the rest of the kids in class. Even if most of them weren't mentally challenged, no offense.

—Eponine cannot learn in a standard class. We do

not have the budget to have an interpreter in class just for her.

—But she reads lips just fine.

—The interpreter wouldn't be for her. How is she going to interact with the teacher when she refuses to speak? A whiteboard?

—But the reason she doesn't speak *is* this class. She was fine until a couple of weeks after school started. If she were in a regular class—

—As I said, Eponine just cannot learn in a standard class.

—But she reads lips *just fine*.

—If Eponine started speaking normally, we would re-evaluate at the end of the school year. From the tone of your voice, you are insinuating that it is *my* fault, *my* poor teaching skills that's behind all her troubles. I'll have you know, I have my Masters and I worked seriously hard for that.

—That's not what I meant at all.

Miss Black glared at me, her breath charging forth from her nostrils. My mind told me to fight on, to accuse her openly of poor teaching, to insult her for being just a teacher, to bring up that those who cannot do, teach, to make fun of her ugly green sweater. I took a breath and tried to calm myself.

—I do respect the work that you do here, I said. —And I know that you are talented, and that you are trying your best, no, I mean, *doing* your best to give my daughter the best education possible. And I thank you for that. I really appreciate that. It's just that this class scares her. It makes her feel different from all the other kids.

—She *is* different from all the other kids. You have got to understand that. I know you want to live in a world where your daughter never has to feel any pain, but that is just not possible.

—But she's so smart.

Miss Black nodded her head in a way that made me think she was only pretending to agree to be polite. She swiveled in her chair, pulled up her email program and sifted through hundreds of emails.

—I have two classes. I teach about twenty kids a year and every week, I get three or more emails from their parents telling me that their child is too smart to be in my class, or that he or she would learn so much better in a "real" class. Imagine how that makes me feel? That they, the parents, will do anything to get their child away from my substandard instruction? I am a real teacher and I work very hard to make sure every child in my class learns as much as they can, which, given the vast range in their abilities, isn't easy. And as to your daughter being so smart, Mr. Bridger.

—James.

—Eponine is cute. She is a good kid. She is smart, but no smarter than any other child her age. I know that is difficult for a parent to hear, that their child is ordinary, but it's true. Eponine is ordinary. She's a fighter, and we'll keep on fighting. Maybe one day, when she starts speaking again, and has fewer behavioral problems, she'll be ready for standard instruction, but until then . . .

She waved her hands in the air, giving the question up to the hypothetical. She turned back and began jotting notes on a worksheet. I stared at her. She looked up again.

—Is there anything else? she asked.

I told her no. I got up and walked out of her office.

12

I waited for Eppy in my car. In the parking lot, an elderly woman with a crossing guard's vest walked by the car several times. I didn't understand why she was doing this or why she gave me judgmental looks out of the corner of her eye until I realized that she probably didn't like the fact that a lone man was waiting for the kids to get out. I thought about leaving the parking lot and driving around until school ended, but there wasn't enough time and it would probably have looked even more suspicious.

The buses lined up in front of the school and the kids poured out of the double doors. I stood by the buses, straining my neck to find my daughter. I shouted her name a few times before remembering she was deaf. Stupid. Finally, I saw her getting ready to get on a bus. I had a horrible vision of her getting on and the bus driving away, but she turned just as her foot touched the first step. When she saw me, she squealed and ran toward me. I felt sorry for the kids she shoved out of the way. She leapt up into my arms and planted kisses on my face.

After we drove home, we both decided that we were bored and wanted to go for a walk around the river. Now this was never the safest thing, even without the hypothermia-producing current that could swallow a grown man whole and spit out a mangled blue corpse.

I took my daughter on these journeys by the waterfront because I couldn't help but be enamored with the way she looked at the world. She was without skepticism, free from the layers of disappointment that build up over the years.

Look at those birds, Daddy, she signed. *Aren't they beautiful?*

—Yes, Eppy, they are very beautiful.

In the distance, white birds chattered amongst the trees. They squawked and played in the cold air. I worried that they were lost and didn't know their way home, that they should get going south else they froze to death.

Look at that fish jump, Eppy signed. *Isn't it beautiful.*

Several feet away, I glimpsed a flash of silver as a trout

splashed in the river. I thought how fish only jumped in the morning—there must have been something wrong with this one. Besides, it was too cold for insects.

—Yes, Eppy. That is beautiful.

Look, a rainbow! That's beautiful!

I followed her finger to where she pointed. In a small bend of the river, in a spot where the rushing water hit a rotting log, there was a whirlpool. In the center of the whirlpool was a slick of oil spinning around. The light bounced off in every color of the rainbow.

—Oh no, Eppy, I said. —That's really bad for the fish.

It is always like this for me. I can no longer think in terms of beauty. It always has to be weighed against the bad things I know. Why could I not see the birds as beautiful without worrying about them being lost? Why could I not see a jumping fish and think about the strength and grace of such an animal without worrying about whether it caught anything?

When I was a child, I absorbed the world with open eyes. There was magic in all I saw. And for what I couldn't see, imagination filled in the rest. Just over the next hill was a castle with banners flying in the wind. Every sleeping dog was secretly a dragon ready to rush into battle.

It is not that I wish to return to childish ways of

thinking. Forcing yourself to not believe the truth through the power of positive thinking is just as destructive as never opening your eyes at all.

It is just that I can no longer see anything, can no longer feel anything without qualifying it with a negative emotion or painful fact. I'll see a bright child dreaming of a career or brilliant future, and can only think how disappointed they are going to be when they discover just how heartless the world is.

I have tried my best to unlearn this habit, but it is hard. I would have to wipe away most everything I've learned. There is no single event that has caused me to think this way. It built up over the years, blow after blow, cut after cut, wound after wound. We step out the door, and a cloud of shrapnel hits us in the face, a burst of negativity and despair we cannot avoid. It has gotten so bad that some days I try not to go outside because I cannot stand being reminded that I am insignificant, that I am a nobody, that truly nobody is anybody, that we are all just trying to finish this sad life, hoping to find some meaning in it all somewhere. It has gotten so bad that I could not tell my daughter that a pool of oil floating on water and throwing rainbows at the air, yes, that was beautiful.

May we find a way to better protect ourselves from

the steel rain of negativity outside our doors. May we grow thick skin so that this steel rain does not bite into us. May we one day pick all the shrapnel from our hearts and look upon the world as new again.

13

I popped into the Oxford for a quick drink before my wife's fundraiser. It was a mistake. I had forgotten it was Griz-Cat weekend, that is, the annual game between the University of Montana and Montana State University. It was a pilgrimage to a holy site of football, at least in this state, with people bundling their entire families up and driving their RVs across the fourth largest state in the U.S. Many didn't even come to watch the game. They just parked their RVs next to the stadium and drank at the tailgates. Festivities started several days before the big game.

I squeezed between two stools and tried to get Mick's attention. Mick liked working at the Oxford because it didn't get slammed compared to the other bars downtown. I could imagine his rage as he raced back and forth, getting drinks for people screaming orders at him.

Each time he ran past, I raised my hand like a guilty pupil.

—Hey, hey man, said a man standing beside me.

He wore a white baseball cap with a torn bill and a blue sweater with the Montana State logo, a snarling bobcat. He had one of those doughy faces that made it difficult to tell his age. He could have been twenty-five or forty. His mouth twisted in drunkenness.

—Hey man, I'm going to stay drunk all weekend.

—Are you really? I said with no interest.

—Yeah, I got here this morning. I said "fuck it" and drove in from Big Sandy this morning. I went into the first bar I found. I've been drinking since nine.

—Good for you.

Mick rushed past but I raised my hand too late.

—I don't know why they call it "Big."

—What?

—Big Sandy. There's like five hundred of us. Hey, you want to drink with me?

—Not particularly. I'm meeting my wife later.

—Just one drink. Whatever you want. I'm buying.

The man in the Bobcat sweater reached into his pocket and pulled out a fistful of sweaty, wadded-up bills. They spilled out of his hands. He reached down to peel the bills off the sticky floor. While he was distracted, I managed to flag down Mick.

—Whiskey Coke.

—You fucking asshole, Mick shouted over the noise. —The whiskey's on the opposite side of the bar. You're going to make me run all that way?

—Rum and Coke.

—Thank you, he said when he came back with my drink. —For being so helpful, you get to pay full price.

He laughed at his joke and sped away. I waited for a moment for my change before deciding that losing a few dollars was more than worth it to not stand next to Mr. Bobcat anymore.

I found Chet sitting at a small table near the jukebox. He was alone, grimacing as a group of college kids in sweaters with fraternity letters kept bumping into him. They crowded around to watch, comment upon and boast about their own prowess in an ongoing poker game. I stood next to the table and leaned against the jukebox.

I turned my head toward Charlie's alcove. Thelma sat there with her new girlfriend. This one was short and thin with dyed blonde hair and a black dress with a frilly collar. She made me think of a Victorian doll. A man in his late twenties tried to talk her up. She smiled disinterestedly with her black-lipsticked lips. Thelma had her mouth open wide with laughter, but that did not hide a look of bitterness, desiring that her girl only talk to her.

—Poor Charlie, I said. —Sad to hear about his stroke.

—Charlie was an asshole, Chet said.

Chet was drunk, and very drunk at that. In the two years that I had been coming to the Oxford, I had never seen him more than a little tipsy. He always kept a good eye on himself and his intake. I wanted to ask him what was wrong and offer any help, but we didn't have that kind of relationship. We could only talk to each other in insults and jests.

—You know the saying that the good die young, Chet said. —Well, he is or at least was living proof that it goes the other way, too.

—You said he got sent to a home, right? He's not dead yet.

—Might as well be dead. Those places are just coffins that they haven't closed the lid on yet.

My mother had stayed a few days in a nursing home while she recovered from her fall down the stairs. I was about to bring up that my mother had been in a home and gotten out, but although technically true, she never got out of bed again.

—You weren't here a decade ago. Charlie used to

come with his wife. This small timid little thing that talked to nobody. It was obvious Charlie was beating the shit out of her night after night. Couldn't prove it. There weren't no bruises showing. She used to sit there all night with him, not saying a word, just stroking his arm from time to time and avoiding eye contact. You got Charlie when he was mellow, not trying to pick a fight with anyone around, knowing that they'd think twice about fighting a seventy-year-old man.

—Why did they let him in if he was so bad?

—Oh, they'd eighty-six him whenever he got bad, but never for good. There were a couple of times that he was supposedly eight-sixed for good, but he'd come in a few weeks later, then it'd be like nothing'd happened.

—That's not right. If he was acting like that, they should have kept him out.

—It's about community. I've got no love for him. I'm glad he's gone. But he's local. Nobody wanted him but he was one of us. After his wife died, I don't know, something broke in him. He didn't want to fight so much. It's kind of sweet in a fucked-up way. But like I said it's about community. He's one of us and we take care of our own. Thelma did his shopping. Mick drove him over to Spokane to the VA hospital every few months. We're a community and we take care of our own. Even if he's a son of a bitch. It's something those in big cities don't understand.

—No, that's not true. I don't think it's got anything to do with cities versus small towns. I remember there was this old Italian guy in our neighborhood. He was schizophrenic as all hell. Racist, too. At first, he seemed a harmless old man, wore nice suits and all, but he'd explode into this storm of screaming racial and homophobic slurs directed at nothing. Most places wouldn't let him in. Even the places that were nicer to him, the ones who'd give him a dollar before sending him right back out the door, had enough of him in his last few years. There was one place, though, this coffee shop that always let him in. They'd give him a cup of coffee, maybe a bite to eat and let him sit at the tables. When he got out of hand, and he always did, they'd kick him out, or on the real bad days call the cops. The next day though, no matter how bad he was the night before, they'd let him back in, give him his coffee, ask him how he was. When he walked in front of the car that broke his spine and sent him to the grave, they had a memorial for him. The owner paid for a funeral procession, with a marching band and the whole works. You'd be surprised how many people came to the funeral. That old bastard would have died alone were it not for that coffee shop.

Chet looked down at the ice in his empty glass and shrugged, as if to say that people were people all over the world, and no one region owned a monopoly on compassion. He pushed his drink over to me.

—Hey, do me a favor. Get a Coke from Mick for me. And get one for yourself. Chug that one first, though.

—Pay up, I said, waving my finger after chugging my rum and Coke. —If you're making me get you a drink, you gotta pay.

—We paid when you forced our kids to give up our language, we paid when . . .

—Okay, Jesus, I said, throwing up my hands and getting out of my chair.

Chet laughed as I walked away. He rolled up his napkin into a ball and threw it at me. When I got Mick's attention, he filled Chet's glass and poured me a draft beer. Mick and I shared a few snippets of what could barely be called a conversation over the noise, and I went back to the table with Chet.

—Mick tells me that your son's going to be on TV.

—Goddamn that asshole, Chet said.

He looked down at his drink with a look that meant he wished he had asked for a whiskey Coke instead of just a Coke.

—Yeah, that's right, Chet admitted.

—Tommy? Shawn?

—No, he grumbled. —The other one.

—Oh, Shadow Wolf.

Chet nodded with a grimace.

—His real name's Christopher. I never told you that, did I?

—Christopher? Oh, my God, Christopher? How drunk were you when you named him that? No one names their kid Christopher, unless they're a dumbass. Wait, I see.

—I'm glad to see you're having your little chuckle at my expense. We can't all have a classy name like you, Bridger. That supposed to mean you build bridges?

—I've thought about changing my name several times, I said. —Only thing is, I don't have that much of an imagination either, so I wouldn't know what to call myself.

—How about "Dickface?"

—Dickface James, I said, scratching my chin. —I like the sound of that. Although I don't know how well that'd go over at a parent-teacher conference.

We laughed at this some more. We suggested names for each other and our kids, each more foul than the last. Finally, the game slowed and the conversation pulled to a stop.

—Well, I'll be over at Red's to watch on Wednesday night. You can come by if you want.

—Am I cordially invited? I laughed. —Do I have to wear a tuxedo?

—Yes, shithead. Here's your ticket.

Chet grabbed up a napkin from the table and stuck it down the front of his pants. He rubbed it around a few times, then pulled it out and threw it on the table. He grinned wildly, the gold of his teeth caps glinting.

—Listen man, I said as I finished my beer. —It's good to see you. I'd stay longer, but I got to get to my wife's fundraiser.

—Good, I was sick of your stupid face anyways. Don't forget your ticket.

He threw the napkin that had been down his pants at my face. It hit me on the mouth and I spat on the floor.

14

I hated my wife's charity events. They always felt awkward and fake, but I stopped trying to convince her to get out of them. We negotiated many compromises to make our two lives work. She, for example, stopped rejecting glasses of wine. Donors had money and their purse strings tightened fast when my wife said that drinking was against her religion. It set her apart, an Other, not a part of their community. My wife then attempted to deceive. She took fake sips of wine, and sought ways to dispose of it, pouring it out in a sink or tipping it discreetly into a planter. During one of her first charity events here, she poured the wine into the pot of a realistic plastic tree. The wine leaked out of the holes in the bottom and out on the floor. I pretended that I, clumsy as I was, had accidentally spilled her wine into the pot.

Her assistants, graduates of the University, would have done fine on their own, but the donors wanted to meet the Director. Their donations were contingent upon their feeling connected to the upper crust of the community, for being patrons of the arts.

I showed up at the gallery an hour into the two-hour event. I had thought about showing up roaring drunk, still dressed in my work clothes. I imagined myself stumbling among the partygoers, relishing the horror in their faces as I pawed their suits and evening gowns with hands still filthy from the day's work. My wife would have no choice but to divorce me after that.

Amanda Carter, one of my wife's assistants, sat just outside the front door with a clipboard. She wore a black dress under a blue down jacket. She was as tall as a volleyball player, with her hair cut short. Small emerald studs glittered in her ears.

—I can't believe my wife is making you stand out in the cold.

—It's not her. It's the gallery owner. He thinks it gives the event more class, makes it more exclusive. It's not so bad. I've got this heater.

She pointed to an electric heater sitting on the pavement to her left. Its red coils glowed with heat.

—You be careful with that thing. You'll end up

half-cooked, I said.

—Don't worry, I'll make someone rotate me every half an hour to make sure. I'm cooked all the way through.

I laughed at this joke, feeling a little displeased that I had not come up with it myself. I made to go inside.

—Just a second, I'm sorry, but I have to make sure you are on the list.

I looked at her, confused. She noticed this and flipped through the clipboard.

—Can't you just say you found me and let me in? You know I belong.

—I'm sorry, but the gallery owner is adamant that we check. He makes us initial.

I helped her flip through the pages until she came across my name. I should have never said anything, as it only made her more flustered. I was never very good at things like that. She found my name in blue ink at the bottom of the list.

Inside the gallery, my wife stood in the center of a knot of people. They were all middle-aged and wearing fine, if not name brand, clothing. I recognized several people among them. One was a local weatherman, another the owner of a sandwich shop. Each in rapture, listening to my wife recount a story about the time she met Chuck Close. I stood to one side until the circle acknowledged me and let me join. Not wanting to break up her story, I leaned in and kissed her on the cheek. Startled, she jumped and looked at me in terror before she smiled and touched my shoulder. I drank from her wine glass to keep her from having to do so herself. There was little to do but wait until the story was finished.

I made to speak when she was done, but the local weatherman jumped in with a story about a fishing trip to Alaska where he tried to describe the sky in terms of a pastel painting. Slowly but surely, the donors pushed me out of the circle. As the story went on, the listeners shifted ever so slightly and I had to shift in response to just be a part of the circle again. Finally, I had enough. I did not come here to be awkward or spend the night laughing false laughter.

I drifted away. No one, including my wife, noticed me. I melted into the scenery and pretended I was interested in the paintings on the wall.

One particularly odd painting caught my eye. It was oppressively brash, with a geometric pink stripe, a black splash of paint, and white stripes.

I could not say if the painting was good. Given the fact that it was hidden in the corner of a small gallery in an obscure city, it probably was not. It was strange to think that the quality of a work of art could often be determined by the wall on which it hung. I looked around for a tag that named the artist and title. I found none. I also looked for a price. If the price was high, that must mean that it was good.

I jumped when I noticed a man standing beside me. He was in his late fifties, with wild hair dyed the wrong color. The roots were a lighter shade of brown mixed with gray. He wore a green suit jacket several sizes too large for him. His mouth hung open and he had a vacant expression.

—Do you like art, sir? the man asked me.

—I guess so. I don't really know about it. My wife, she knows a lot. I know nothing about art.

—Just because you haven't read those books that try to tell you what art is, and will say that you're wrong if you think otherwise, doesn't mean you don't know art. I mean, you feel something when you look at a painting. Some paintings, that is. Only a few.

—I do.

—That's good. I can never trust somebody that likes all art. It means they are merely saying they think they are cultured. Tell me, sir. Do you like this painting?

—I do.

—I'm not necessarily sure I believe you. But as you don't know that I am, in fact, the artist, I cannot say it is on account of sycophancy.

—You painted this?

—I did. Many years ago.

—It is nice. I am just saying I don't really like art, but this is nice.

I waited for the artist's reaction. Part of me was angry at myself for praising the work. Knowing that this was his painting changed things. Lord knows I've said empty words to many people when they shared a story or showed me something they had made.

—It is because of this work that I stopped painting. I gave up all art, in fact.

The unexpected response froze my lips. We stood together in awkwardness for several more minutes.

—In my head, the painting was perfect. Oh god, was it perfect, the artist said, true emotion creeping into his voice for the first time. —I could never forgive myself that this painting did not live up to the one in my head. This is not the worst painting I have ever done. But when I look at it, I can only see what it could have been. I despise this painting.

—I suppose I could have gotten better, he continued after a long pause. —I could have developed more skill, or attempted another version, but it's done now. I do like to come every so often and look at it, to remind myself as a kind of *memento mori*. I am glad no one has bought it yet.

—May I ask how much you are selling it for?

—Oh, I don't know. The owner must be selling it for two thousand, given the prices on the placards next to the rest of the failures in here. All art is failure, don't you know? It never lives up to what the artist intends to express. It can never be that arc of lighting across the void that brings true human connection.

I thought about it. I remembered the four thousand left in my wife's and my joint checking account. There would be no way I could justify the expense. A part of me told me to buy it anyway, if only to make the artist like me, and to feel that his work was not a failure.

The man turned to leave. He had a slow, lumbering gait that made me think of someone walking out to his death among the ocean waves. I called out to him.

—What's the name of this piece?

The artist turned slowly. On his lips was a wry smile.

—Oh, I've quite forgotten it.

He left. I turned back to the painting and looked at it. My mind did more calculations, and figured out ways to move money around to afford it, and how to hide the painting once I had purchased it. I thought how ridiculous it would be to spend so much money just to hide the thing from my wife.

Then, something odd happened. The piece of art changed in my mind so that it was just a painting. It was pretty to look at, nothing more.

I looked around the room just in time to see my wife head to the back of the gallery. She wore a smile and nodded to those she passed, but I had lived with her long enough to read her face. I headed in back to be with her.

I found her leaning over a sink in the back. The sink was one of the metal kinds with deep reservoirs used to wash tools. Her breathing was rapid and shallow.

On the counter was a small lunch bag. I grabbed it and gave it to her. My wife put it over her mouth and hyperventilated into it. I could do nothing more. I didn't know how to do anything more.

—You should let Amanda take over for you. She's probably freezing to death out in the cold.

My wife did not answer. I thought she might have nodded, but that might just have been her erratic breathing.

—You made it longer this time than the last, I said. —The last charity event, you didn't last half an hour.

It's too bad you couldn't work behind the scenes like at your old job and you wouldn't have to stress yourself out with so many people.

I didn't say what I was thinking: *It's too bad I forced you out of your old job at a museum you liked to come to this place.*

—Do you know that painting in the corner? The one that's got no tag? I think I like it. I was even thinking about buying it. That's if you're okay with us starving to death just to have something to hang on the wall.

I laughed. It was a feeble laugh. It didn't cheer her up.

When she found her breath again, I helped her into her coat and we said our goodbyes to the donors and the gallery owner. I lied and said that it was I who was not feeling well, to spare my wife's pride. I noticed the confusion registering on some of the donors' faces as they struggled to remember who I was and why I was taking the Director away with me.

We relieved Amanda from her post and I stood on the street corner while my wife gave her unnecessary instructions. Then we walked home.

15

That night I had a vivid dream, and when I awoke, I found it difficult to believe in the world that presented itself before my eyes. I did not want to leave the dream, but when I closed my eyes again, I could not find the way back. I sat up on the edge of the bed and searched for a piece of paper and a pen to write down the details of the dream, but when I found them, the images were already gone. I sat there with a profound sense of loss.

I dressed and showered. Downstairs on the stove were last night's leftovers. I ate, the spicy stew hurting my stomach. I turned on the television, but it just confused me and I turned it off after several minutes.

Feeling fresh air and a bit of work would be good, I went outside and began clearing away some of the dead branches in the backyard.

It wasn't until I turned that I saw my wife in the attic

window. Up there, in a space converted into a cramped study, she picked up her special silver pen and began writing something.

In the second year of our marriage, the two of us took a trip to Berlin. I say the two of us, but Eppy was a stowaway in my wife's womb. My wife had wanted to see her old professor, who was dying of emphysema. I would like to say that I was seduced by the old city. After all, here in America, we have no sense of age. Something that was built in the 1800s is almost unimaginably old, whereas in Europe, you can walk among temples built before the advent of written language. The Brandenburg Gate was nice. That was all the emotion that viewing the triumphal arch implanted in me. Dom Berlin was nice. I was too closed off to appreciate anything anymore. I wanted to visit the museum at which my wife had once worked. It was closed for renovation, however, and I refused to let my wife pull any strings to get us in. At first, I had told myself that the answer would most certainly be "no" and I didn't want to risk her getting chewed out by the art director. It took me a couple of years to realize I was embarrassed and intimidated. I was little more than a random man off the street being let into one of the sacred spaces of art. Most likely, she had wanted to spend one more day with her paintings and I had stolen that from her.

My wife and I visited her old professor on the third day we were in Berlin. His name was Claude Hinkel. From what my wife told me, he had been instrumental in her attaining a position at that museum. I expected a man who sat every morning in his country garden with a glass of white wine and a purebred Weimaraner at his feet. I expected a library with shelves cracking under the weight of leather-bound tomes. I expected an antique globe containing a hidden minibar that would reveal skinny bottles of schnapps if one knew the correct country to push.

Instead, Dr. Hickel lived in a one-bedroom apartment in a part of Berlin called Lichtenberg. The dying man sat in a folding chair in the kitchen, resting spindly arms on a shoddy Formica table. The kitchen was so cramped it was uncomfortable for just us three. His bedroom door was open. Through it I could see a small dresser and an unmade single bed. Above the bed was a charcoal drawing of a female nude in an obscene pose. The smell of urine wafted in through the door.

Despite all the weakness in the thin man—his skin so pale it was almost translucent—I saw he still possessed the singular emotion of fury. When my wife and

I first arrived, he gave me a look of contempt that shattered my view of the relationship between him and my wife. It was not, as I had been led to believe, one of respect and dignity, of free exchange between peers, or of the composed teacher imparting knowledge upon the eager but inferior youth. Theirs was a relationship of dominance. He detested her. He detested her talent and he detested the fact that, although she was no longer young, he would be dead before he saw her broken.

The professor smiled suddenly. My wife sat at the other chair on the kitchen table and chatted with her former mentor. They spoke in English at first, out of respect for me, but as soon as it became clear that everything they had to talk about did not include me, they switched to German. I went out on the balcony that adjoined the kitchen to get some fresh air.

The balcony looked out on a small park. The apartments surrounding it were built of plain unadorned stone. Below, a group of children played with a soccer ball, while another group chased each other and screamed in excitement. Seeing this, I had a feeling that we hadn't gone on a trip at all, that we had only driven across town, and if my wife was going to stay a while and chat with her professor, I might as well walk home.

Perhaps this should have led to an epiphany about the interconnectedness of humankind, how everywhere around the world people's lives were essentially the same. Instead, I felt that I had been tricked. I had spent so much money to come here, and everything looked the same. It was almost as if the airline had taken our money, had flown around in a circle for thirteen hours and had landed on the other side of town. This feeling—that God designed the world specifically against us—we entertain as teenagers, reject as young adults, but cannot quite shake for the rest of our lives.

Later, after it had begun to rain, I went back inside. Before we could make our final goodbyes, the professor asked us in English to visit a department store to pick up some items. He said that the neighbor who shopped for him spoke poor German, got the wrong things, and always tried to screw him over the change. My wife wrote these down using a silver pen taken from his table.

The professor's demands were not demanding. All he wanted was some printer paper, a pack of fresh underwear, and other odds and ends. When we returned to the apartment, the professor was furious. We had not even gotten in the door when he leaped to his feet and launched profanity after profanity at my wife. He slipped between German and English, so that I could only pick up half of what he was saying. Not that I wanted to know. He called her a plagiarist, ungrateful, and—every man's favorite insult for women—a whore. My wife looked at him with an unsurprised face, even as she backed away and out of the apartment. The professor lurched forward, his red eyes burning, spittle running down his screaming mouth. He braced himself against the wall while he gulped air into his emphysematous lungs. Then he knocked the shopping bag out of my wife's hands. The doors along the corridor cracked open. His neighbors peered out of them to watch the commotion. With this new audience for whom to create a scene, the professor kicked the shopping bag down the hall, loosing a shower of candy, paper and clean underwear everywhere.

On our plane ride back to the United States, my wife was searching through her purse for a mint when she found the silver pen. She never sent it back. It was not that she forgot. This was a woman with a memory like a bear trap, who could remember nearly every detail about someone she had just met. She was not a selfish woman with a "finders, keepers" mindset. She had once chased a woman six blocks to return a ten-dollar bill that had fallen out of the woman's purse. Refusing to return the pen was perhaps the one revenge against her professor that she allowed herself to take.

16

Monday morning, I headed into work to find that I had only one scheduled job. I was happy. I was even happier to find that the job was in Missoula, and I didn't have to spend the whole day driving back and forth. Why did this woman have a septic tank when she could have just hooked up to the main sewage lines? I didn't know, but I wasn't going to complain.

I pulled up to the house twenty minutes later. It was old and had not been built by the most precise of hands. Latticework and decorative whorls were a half-hearted attempt to enliven its dreary façade. The builder must have seen a Victorian house once and attempted to copy the style. The roof sagged. Squirrels ran back and forth across it, their cheeks swollen with nuts.

Twisting ceramic sculptures filled the front yard. It was hard to tell what these sculptures were supposed to be. Were they good? Bad? I didn't know. My wife might.

I knocked on the front door, not being able to find the doorbell. After three tries with no answer, I made a note in my log that the woman customer was not home and made my way back to the truck to get a paper to stick to the door saying that I had come and would return at such and such time. While I was halfway across the yard, I heard a voice.

—You're the guy, right?

I turned to see a woman, probably in her mid-forties. She had brown hair sprinkled with gray. Her lipstick was bright red, and she wore blue denim coveralls. On top of her head was a pair of safety goggles secured with an elastic band. She smiled and waved at me.

—The guy from the place? she asked.

—Yes. Yes, I am.

—Well, come on back. I was just about to do some carving.

I followed her to a backyard surrounded on all sides with thick foliage. The yard was small, but intimate and cut off from everything else. If I had a place like this, I could forget that the outside world even existed. There was a cedar porch with furniture. Vines, naked now that it was winter, climbed up the herringbone trellises. In the far corner of the backyard, a tree drooped with heavy branches. Under that was another small sitting area with two wooden chairs and a small table in front of a fire pit. In the middle of the yard was a five-foot-tall log stood on one end. Next to that was an orange and black chainsaw.

—You're going to need these, she said, handing me a set of blue earplugs.

She showed me where the sewage tank was, and it did not take long to dig for the access cover. The sculptor started up the chainsaw. It chugged and whined as she hacked away at the log. I hooked up the piping to the septic tank, then sat in a wooden chair below the willow tree and watched her work. The sculptor attacked the log, alternating between the chainsaw and a series of rasps. Soon, she coaxed the shape of a bear out of the wood. Finished, she put her tools down, shook the sawdust out of her hair and packed her tools up and into a shed. Then she came up to me where I was sitting.

—You look like a coffee man, she said.

—I would say that I am.

—Sit tight for a few minutes, and I'll make some.

I did not have to wait long. The sculptor brought out a French press filled with steaming coffee, along with two cups. The coffee was especially good, as were the pecan bars that she also brought. The air was a bit chilly, so she brought some wood and newspaper and built a small fire.

—Well, what do you think? she asked, tipping her cup toward the wooden bear.

—It's very good.

—It's shit, the sculptor said. —These wooden bears are so cheesy, but they're well-paying cheese. I could sell a couple of these a week if I really tried. People can't seem to get enough of them.

—You do see them everywhere.

—Us Montanans, we're so predictable. You from Montana?

I said that I was.

—You look at the people here, they all dress alike, they all talk alike. Like the men, they always wear a ball cap with a pair of sunglasses on the bill. Either than, or the sunglasses are upside down and hanging on the back of their head. Everyone wears a flannel shirt or fleece from North Face or some company like it. And Carhartt. Carhartt everywhere.

I looked down at my own Carhartt jacket and pants.

—I think a lot of Montanans try so hard to be Montanans, she said.

—It's like that everywhere. People want to belong

to something. Clothing's a simple way to show it. It's easy to buy, just like the statues they keep on their front porches.

—It doesn't bother me that much, but yes. And if they keep buying my stuff, I don't care how bland their culture is. That's the artist's dilemma, right? Whether to make the art you want or make what sells.

—How about find the place that buys that work that you want to make?

The sculptor threw back her head and filled the backyard with laughter.

—I spent the first twenty years of my life doing that. I can tell you that it doesn't exist. No, about five years ago, I gave up and started learning how to do chainsaw sculptures. The remnants, the autopsy, you could say, of my artistic aspirations lie in my front yard.

—Those? Those are . . .

The sculptor cocked a flirty eyebrow. She smiled with one corner of her mouth.

—You better say that they're good. Otherwise you'll hurt my feelings. Just kidding. No, I've realized that I'm just not very good. That was difficult to accept, so so hard. But what can we do? Give up or keep trying. Nobody can call any art good unless it's been around for fifty years or more. People say you have to wait until the artist dies, but I think it takes longer. It's got to become an artifact. People look at a Warhol not to get an insight into his life but the crazy weirdness of the sixties. Do you like art?

—Me? No. My wife does. She runs the art museum downtown.

—Oh, I know her! I've met her many times. The little hussy won't show any of my artwork. I'm sorry. That's your wife. I did not offend you, I hope. I say stupid things. She's a good woman. Smart as a whip. She's made the museum so much better. The only problem is that shitty artists like me get left out in the cold.

—I worry for her, I said. —I feel she's way too good for this small city. The museum must look like it's filled with the drawings of children compared to the collections she used to curate.

—She's got a good eye. If there's a hidden master to be found somewhere in these woods and mountains, it'll be her who finds them. Besides, don't knock Missoula too much. Good paintings are more than the names attached to them.

—I could talk to her for you, I said. —Convince her to take on a few of your—

—Nope, no way. I will not hear it. I remember

inviting her over once a few months ago. She was very nice to me about my work, but I could tell that's what it was, being nice. That hurt a lot, I'd have to admit. It would have been better if she had just told me that they were garbage and left. That way I could at least convince myself that I was a tortured, underestimated artist pushed down by the system. But telling me that they were good in order not to hurt my feelings made me feel like a child. Like I haven't learned anything in my thirty years of doing them. Excuse me. Just thinking about it gets me a bit teared up. No. Do not ask her to show my work. Even if she changed her mind, I'd worry that she's just being nice to me again. It's okay. In fact, it was good. I had a bit of an epiphany about that a few days later. Realizing that I was mediocre freed me. I no longer had to worry about being a great artist, I was free to do what I wanted. I no longer felt guilty doing these chainsaw sculptures. I no longer felt I was giving up, I no longer hated them. It's a lot like men, I think. How's that for a segue? I've been divorced like five times now. I always had a knack for picking men that didn't want to stick around. No, that's not right. That's a lie that I tell myself. The greatest ability of the human mind is the ability to deceive itself, that's what one of my ex-husbands used to say. No, my husbands did not leave me. I made their lives so difficult that they had no choice. They did so, I think because I made them feel that they were not good enough for me. That I had hoped for a Prince Charming and had ended up with a loser. I was suckered into this true love bullshit they teach girls. True love might have meant something hundreds of years ago, when traveling to other towns was so difficult, and if you're going to marry anybody, you're going to end up marrying someone else around your home. Maybe it was a help to these girls married off at thirteen years old. Maybe it made a girl feel better as she struggled to breathe under the weight of her new husband, a man she did not know and was thirty years older, that she had met her true love. After all, in some cultures, this is the only man she's ever met outside of her family. These days, where meeting a new person is as easy as downloading a smartphone app. When we can travel around the world in half a day. How am I supposed to find my one true love in all that? What if my one true love is a yak farmer in Nepal, right? But I'm sorry. I talk too much. Do you want some more coffee? No, don't wave it off. I can't believe we drank the whole pot. But I'll make a fresh batch. Don't go sneaking off while I'm gone.

The sculptor disappeared into her house. I got up

and stretched. Although it was warm next to the small fire, the cold seeped in everywhere, and I needed to get some movement in my joints. I went over to the bear sculpture. Even in its raw shape, I could tell that the woman had talent. It was true that one saw these chainsaw sculptures everywhere in this town, but this one was made by an artist who knew form. It had life and movement in its playfully extended paws. The door opened and the woman came out carrying another pot of coffee and a tray of snacks.

—Hey, I told you not to run away, she said. —Just kidding.

I smiled and went back to the wooden chair. Instead of pecan bars, she had little tea cookies coated with powdered sugar. They were soft and chewy and I had to brush the sugar off my jacket with every bite.

—What were we saying? Oh, yes. We were talking about love right? I got a new man. We've been dating for a few weeks now. He'll come by in another couple of hours and be really jealous that you're here. He's in love with me, or at least he thinks he's in love. Honestly, I think a couple can never say they're in love until they've been married forty years or more. You see these old couples who do nothing but bicker, but they cannot live without each other. The "ego," if you will, the sense of self, melts and you are not sure where you end and your loved one begins.

I lied to her and said I agreed. My mother and father were certainly not in love. They didn't bicker. Maybe that was the mistake. Had they bickered, like I used to do with my wife, maybe my mother would have been much happier. Maybe she wouldn't have built that wall around herself to try to keep her hopes pure from the ocean of disappointment outside it, a wall that often excluded me, a young boy who would tell jokes and sing silly songs in an attempt to make her happy.

We must forgive our parents for the mistakes they made when they raised us. My mother tried the best she could to raise me, she just went about it the wrong way. I too often pushed my own will on my daughter. I tried to mold her into the form I wanted and felt like a failure when she resisted.

Sitting in the garden, I had the realization that I could forgive my mother. She simply did not know any better. It would not be easy. The bitterness that she put in me and that I had duplicated tenfold would not be easy to extract. But with her death, I was the only person that could do a fucking thing about it.

—I wish I knew this when I was twenty years old, the sculptor continued. —When I was twenty, I thought I was so wise. Ten years later, when I was thirty, I realized how dumb I was. Ten years after that, well, I'm not going to go on and reveal just how old I am, but know how it's going to go. If I keep this up, I'll probably end up the wisest person alive.

—I don't think it works that way, I said.

—Well, that's going to be what I choose to believe. Remember, the most powerful ability of the human mind is the ability to deceive itself, right? Hold on. I think I hear my boyfriend's car.

From the driveway came the sound of a car pulling in and an engine stopping. The sculptor helped me roll up the hoses and put everything away. Her boyfriend came in back and we three talked. He was a short man with a broad chest and a crew cut. He wore a business suit with a loose gray tie. He introduced himself and even offered a hand to shake, which I waved off due to my dirty hands. He smiled, but I could see a smidgen of jealousy in his eyes. From the glittering joy in the sculptor's eyes, I knew that he had nothing to worry about.

17

I needed to sit and think. After the liveliness of the sculptor, I doubted I could go home and deal with all that sadness. I got a cup of coffee to go and pulled into a department store parking lot along Reserve Street. I reached behind the seat for a manila envelope and shook out a stack of papers bundled with a rubber band. The rubber band was near its breaking point and I made a note to buy a larger one.

My wife could never stand idle hands. When she was not writing in connection to her work, she was writing letters. When she was not writing letters, she was cooking dinner. When she was not cooking dinner, she was brushing our daughter's mane of wild brown hair. Those rare times when she could not find something else for her hands to do, she drew.

Her favorite subject was the male nude. Such was

her talent that with only a few strokes of her pen, she could evoke the most realistic portraits I had ever seen erupt from the human hand. She scribbled minor masterpieces on grocery receipts and in the margins of the newspaper. Young and beautiful men shared the same importance as the obese and ugly. She would draw an achingly beautiful Adonis reclining on a rock in one drawing, and a dying old man with jutting ribs like signposts to the end of his life in another. The one common trait among all of them was that every man was bald. It could be she only found beauty in the bald head—maybe I should give up on the thinning patch on top of my head. She might love me again. Or, perhaps, she was just shit at drawing hair.

My wife held no value in these sketches. Perhaps, when she worked at the finest of museums, co-workers had seen these and scoffed at her amateur hand. Perhaps she only valued drawings if they were a hundred years old and behind glass. I used to collect her sketches and organize them into a file, but when my wife found them, she threw them away. Once there was a quiet war between us, me distracting her to slip a receipt from her grasp, her tossing it, me checking the garbage on trash day, looking for the remnants. Now I believed this war to be over. I had my little collection behind the seat of my work truck. This was risky. It would strain the credibility of my heterosexuality among my coworkers if Trevor or the maintenance guys found this packet full of pictures of naked men in my truck, but it was the only place where I knew my wife would never find them. I took three new portraits from my inner coat pocket. She had sketched them the night before to calm her nerves before she went to bed. I slipped them in with the others.

Even with the coffee, I felt sleepy. After I returned the packet to its hiding place behind the seat, I told myself I would take a quick nap for fifteen minutes or so. When my toes first dipped into the waters of sleep, I laughed to myself, knowing it was a lie.

It was dark when I pulled into headquarters. The parking lot was abandoned. I checked the clock. Maureen was going to be furious. Telling the truth, that I had taken a nap on company time, wouldn't fly. If I had had several jobs that day, I could have said that each one had run a little long. There would be no need to double check. But since I'd had only one job, I'd have to say that something had gone seriously wrong and caused a delay. Maureen would have to call up the customer to see if there were any damages to pay or if the company could just get by with offering a discount.

I waited in the truck, cooking up a good story that didn't involve calls to or from the customer. A dim light shone through the windows. I sighed. I could not lie to Maureen; the best thing was to tell the truth. That I was late because I spent hours chatting with a client, and then took a nap in a parking lot. She could fire me for that. I didn't think she would. I didn't imagine, if she could put up with Trevor all these years, that this incident would be the one to put her over the edge—but it meant my name would slip off the Winter List.

Deciding it was best to get it over with, I left the truck and headed to the office. I was surprised to find Laura, not Maureen, sitting alone at her desk. Her computer was off and she was reading a book under her office lamp.

—You're in late, she said with a smile.

—Yes, I uh, I said, searching for some sort of lie.

—Talking too much with one of the customers, right? I knew it. Who was it? Was it a girl? Was she prettier than me? Laura laughed. —I can already answer that one for you. No girl is prettier than me.

—No, she wasn't.

—I knew it. You missed the drama today.

—What's that?

—Trevor came back, begged for his job. The guy

was crying. We eventually had to call the cops on him.

—I would say "poor guy," but I won't.

—That's right. But, my mother has one soft spot in her cold little heart and she hired him again.

—Shit.

—He won't be on the Winter List, though.

—Well, I guess we'll spend the winter out together. I already got one write-up, and I'll get another one for today.

—You just can't help yourself. You got one of those faces that makes people want to talk to you. Problem is, you listen.

—What is one of those faces that people want to talk to? What do they look like?

—Lumpy, like a pile of fresh dough, she laughed.

—Aw, I said, —I'm a bit more handsome than that.

I stroked my cheeks and pursed my lips like a male model. Laura put down her book and approached me. She kneaded my face like it was dough in her hands. We both laughed and she planted a warm kiss on my cheek.

—Let me show you something.

She took my hand and led me to a toolbox next to the door. She selected a black-handled Philips screwdriver, then led me to the time clock.

—Don't tell anyone I know how to do this.

She lifted up the cover and worked on the clock with the screwdriver. She reset it to read 3:15, then closed the cover again. She motioned to my timecard.

—I don't know, I said. —I don't want to get in trouble.

—Oh, poor baby. How old are you?

She grabbed my card and punched it before I could grab it. She handed it back. I rubbed it between my fingers as if it were somehow unholy.

—I've done it lots of times, Laura said. Don't worry. I'm not stealing. I don't like to sit at home sometimes, so I just stay in at work. I forget to clock out, and my mom gets real mad, saying she can't afford to pay overtime. So, I learned up how to change it. I can clock out whenever I want and mom won't get mad.

She poked around the time clock with the screwdriver again and set it back to the correct time.

—If you're wondering, my mom wasn't here at 3:15. She was dealing with Trevor, so I can say you came in when she was out.

—I don't like you lying for me. Besides, my car was here.

—She won't notice. As long as your timecard says a halfway reasonable number, it'll be fine.

I slipped it back into its slot. I wasn't sure I could trust her, and I could start to feel the lean of this slippery slope. The next time I walked in late, if Laura suggested a timecard change, I'd be less resistant.

—You have plans? You going straight home? she asked.

—I hadn't thought about it. Eppy is at a friend's house and I don't know if I can bear all that silence from my wife. I was just planning on going to the bar.

—Oh, so predictable.

—You want to get something to eat together, maybe go to your place later?

—My place is so boring. Come here. Give me your hand.

She led me to the chair in front of her computer. She straddled me with her legs, kissing my mouth and taking off her shirt. Her nipple was hot and warm in my mouth. She breathed shallow and fast. Moans escaped from the bottom of her throat. Sitting there, I felt I would never understand female sexuality. Men, all we care about is our dicks. It is not that there are no other erogenous zones on a man's body, but that one area overpowers everything. Laura, however was in ecstasy, rubbing her crotch against mine and delighting at the touch as I passed my hand along her back. Then she pushed me back and pulled off her pants and underwear, leaning over the desk. She grabbed the back of my head and forced it into her. I licked and sucked, intoxicated by her scent. Excitement and paranoia rippled through me that her mother might come back to the office at any moment. Laura orgasmed hard. She could not support herself on her quivering legs. We made room for her on the desk, and we made love there. Then we went to the showers in the back and cleaned up, each struggling to keep our hands off one another. Afterwards we got Chinese takeout and went back to her place. The food stayed uneaten on the counter and we went directly into the bedroom and made love several more times.

I did not stay the night, getting home minutes before the sun peeked over the horizon. I think that was a line that I was still not ready to cross.

18

The week passed quickly. Every time I stood next to my wife I worried she would say something about the smell of another woman on my body. Either she did not smell anything, or she did and said nothing about it. She did not say anything when I went back to Laura another two times. I was guilty, yes. The guilt ripped through like a knife every time I saw my wife. A little guilt is nothing compared to the pain my wife would feel when she found out. Far less than what Eppy would feel.

Wednesday rolled around, and I went to Red's Bar to drink with Chet and watch his son on the news. I ordered a drink from the bartender, a thin woman with curly hair, wrinkled skin and a brace around her left wrist. She flirted with me, saying, "What can I get you, love?" And "Anything else, dear?" Also at the bar was a forty-year-old man in a duster jacket. He was bald, with small eyes behind thin spectacles. His prominent underbite and fleshy lips made him look like a bulldog. My wife would have found something beautiful in this face, and one day his naked body would stare out at me from a crumpled receipt or magazine clipping. At the other end of the bar sat an elderly man with bushy eyebrows and a crushed cowboy hat. His red-rimmed eyes were sad, and his left hand shook between drinks. He must have been this bar's Charlie. In the corner of the room, staring at a flat-screen television, was Chet on his scooter.

—I thought I smelled something terrible when I walked past the front door, I said.

—Huh? What?

He looked up at me with confused eyes. He blinked twice.

—Chet, it's me, I said.

—Oh. Sorry. My blood sugar's been a little low these past few days. I think my pump may be on the fritz.

He reached under his shirt and pulled out the insulin pump. Two tubes jutting out of the device sank into Chet's body. He flicked it with his finger several times.

—I'm sorry. I didn't mean to bust your balls.

—I understand. You're probably just curious because you don't have balls of your own.

I laughed a cathartic laugh. It was good to see that he was still able to sling an insult.

—Your son on yet?

—Not for another twenty minutes.

—I see that you don't have a drink in front of you. That, sir, is a problem.

—No. I've got to cut back, he said, adjusting his blanket to where his right leg used to be. —My doctor's been on my ass to quit.

—Your doctor a mountain climber or something? He's got to be to get on top of your huge ass.

He looked at me funny.

—Sorry, I said. —I tried too hard for that one. What I'm trying to say is that you're fat.

—I'd rather be fat than be a pussy. Now, go get me a drink, pussy.

—Rum and Coke?

—Whisky ditch.

—You sure?

—On second thought, I'll have a whiskey ditch, California-style. That's where you give the water to a rich man instead.

I laughed and went back to the bar to order a straight shot of whiskey. The bartender poured it into a small plastic cup. When I sat down, I started in on the jokes again, but all were as lame as before. I was beginning to think I was losing it. Then I remembered that I had never had it. Chet's responses to my jokes were half-hearted. That made me try harder to tell even worse jokes. He stared at the TV while I dug myself a deeper hole.

—Don't tell me you're nervous, I said. —Are you?

—What? No, fuck you.

—Your son will do fine, Chet.

—That's not it. That's not it at all.

I gave up trying to get him into a better mood, and grabbed a set of darts from the bar. I hadn't shot darts in a while and I couldn't hit anything. So, I mostly just messed around, happy that the bar was near empty and I didn't make a fool of myself. I added more than a few extra holes to the wall. I heard the program start and brought my darts and beer to Chet's table.

A graphic washed the television screen, followed by images of Native Americans, mostly culled from movies, dressed in traditional garb dancing around a fire or on white horses charging across the plains. Juxtaposed with this were clips from sporting events. White men with face paint dressed up in feathers ran around basketball courts and swung large foam tomahawks on football fields. I saw the lines around Chet's mouth tighten.

The intro dissolved into a broadcast of a brown-haired white man tucked into a tailored gray suit. Next to him was another white man, so similar in looks that the two men could have been brothers, except that the second one had blonde hair and wore a blue suit. They both sat on a gray sofa with a fake New York skyline behind it. Sitting on a burgundy armchair a few feet away was a young Native American man. His thick black hair hung down in two long braids on either side of his face. He wore a buttoned-up shirt and tie, which looked completely out of place on him. He smiled weakly, a little dazzled by the lights.

—Welcome back to the program. I'm Jacob Laramie, and you know my co-host Allen Caesar. This is the second hour of the Laramie Session. We're going to switch gears from politics and shift to the red-hot debate of Native American mascots in sports.

—I don't see what the big deal is, the one called Caesar said, flashing his perfect white teeth. —I really don't.

—Joining us tonight is an activist and blogger from Missoula, Montana, who *does* see what the big deal is. Please welcome our very special guest, Christopher Fogerty, that is, Christopher "Shadow Wolf" Fogerty.

—Thank you, I'm happy to be here, said Shadow

Wolf, bowing his head.

—Now Chris, can I call you Chris? Laramie asked.

—Goddammit, Chet said as he drank his whiskey. —Here it starts.

—Actually, I would rather you use my professional moniker. In the 1800s, settlers gathered up Native American children and converted them forcibly to Christianity, so—

—I'm going to have to stop you there, said Laramie. —We don't really have the time for a history lesson here. What we are here to discuss is: what is your beef with sports mascots?

—I like his traditional dance he does every game, said Caesar. —I think it's pretty cool.

—That's not a traditional dance, though, Shadow Wolf said. —It's something dreamed up by—

—Now, my last name is Laramie, and I've done some research and I found out that it is a Crow tribal name. So, I have some native in me as well, and it doesn't offend me. Why should it offend me and I'm part Indian? In fact, a recent study discovered that seventy-five percent of Native Americans are not offended by nicknames such as these. Should we stop everything just because of a small minority?

—Well, you're talking about the Connecticut

Report. The thing about that report is—

—It is my understanding, said Caesar, —that teams choose mascots that strike fear into the hearts of the opposing team. They are intimidating and strong. I don't know, but I'd think I'd be proud of that. Aren't you proud of that? Don't you feel proud that your people are strong?

—You don't understand. Native Americans aren't—

—Now your blog, shadowwolfprints.com, let's get a graphic up there for those of you at home, Laramie said. —Go ahead and visit yourself. Your blog gets what thirty, forty hits a month? I do believe you have a YouTube channel that does a little better.

—I'd like to answer Mr. Caesar's question if I can, Shadow Wolf said.

—Just a moment. Now your top YouTube video, I believe, only reached a total of 300 views. Do we have an exact number? I see. 317 on a sheet of paper my producer is holding. Yes, 317. Thanks, Jimmy. You're the best.

—And some of those are people watching it twice or three times, Caesar said.

—Please let me answer a question.

—I'm asking you a question. Now, if you're getting video views in the low hundreds and the games featuring teams with these mascots are getting viewership in the millions, it's very difficult for me to see this as a legitimate issue. If this were a legitimate issue, wouldn't your videos be extremely popular? Wouldn't major news networks cover it all the time?

—It is a legitimate issue. We have been trying to speak about it for a very long time, but whenever we try to speak about it, we get cut—

—I'm going to have to stop you there. We've got to turn it over for a commercial break. When we come back, we're going to read some of your tweets and gauge your reaction at home, so send those messages in, hashtag LaramieSession. And a special thanks to our guest. After that, we've got a video of a cat with brain freeze that you have just got to see.

—Turn it off, Chet growled.

—It's not over. Maybe they'll have more to say, who knows?

—Turn. It. Off.

—That was painful to watch. They bullied him, but I think he got his point across. Well, no, but he got his foot in the door. At least there'll be more and more people headed to his website. That's actually good for him.

Chet's face twisted in fury.

—There's no more. Turn it the fuck off.

I walked up to the television and searched the side for the power button. I couldn't find it.

—Hey, bartender, I shouted. —Can you turn this off? Do you have a remote?

—Hold on, I have one here, the bartender said, sifting through a drawer behind the bar.

—Listen Chet, that guy Laramie's an asshole. Everyone knows it. Christopher had to expect that kind of treatment when he agreed to be on the show.

—Here, I got it, the bartender said as she flipped the channel to a sports station.

—I didn't say to fucking change the channel, you cunt! I want it off.

—I ain't turning it off. It's my bar, it's my rules. You don't like what's on, you leave.

—Jesus, Chet, I said. —Calm down.

Chet downed the rest of his whiskey in one gulp. He threw the plastic cup at the TV screen. Before I could grab him, he threw my half-drunk beer at the screen. The glass shattered against the wall and beer and foam splashed in the corner.

—That's it, you fucker, the bartender shouted. —You're eighty-sixed, you Indian piece of shit.

—He's just pissed is all, I pleaded. —He just

watched his son get destroyed on live TV.

—I don't care. He just tried to destroy my property and I take that very seriously. Now if you don't get your teepee-creeping ass out of here, I'm calling the cops.

The man in the duster stood up. He stared up at us like he was bar security.

—Sit down, Max. I can handle this, the bartender said.

The man in the duster did not sit down. He cracked his knuckles.

—And what the fuck are you supposed to do, fag-boy? Chet shouted at the man in the duster. —You got the guts to come over here?

—Get out, or I'm calling the cops, last chance, the bartender croaked.

—Let's just get out of there, I pleaded. —No sense in taking this too far.

—Get your hands off my chair, you fucking white motherfucker. Fuck all of you, Chet shouted in my face.

—It's shitty. I agree that what they did on TV is shitty. Let's just get out of here. Let's go to the Oxford, okay?

—I wish I had my knife and I'd just cut that white face off your skull.

Chet was immovable. Eventually, he shut up, but

still refused to move. He sat there, brimming with anger, and gripping the side of his wheelchair. The bartender hurled more abuse at him, but it didn't get much worse than what had already been said. She called the cops while the man in the duster glared.

There was nothing to do except for wait. Two fresh-faced police officers arrived. Their uniforms looked straight from the dry cleaners. One had red hair and the last name of Poole across his nametag. The other, with black hair, was named Blunt. Poole leaned over and put his hands on the table.

—What seems to be the problem, Sitting Bull?

Chet did not respond.

—We were watching television, I started to say.

—Hold on there, Blunt said. —We know how to deal with these folk.

—You get a little firewater in them, Poole said, grinning, —they think they're on the warpath again. Now can you tell me happened, Crazy Horse?

Again, I tried to tell what happened, and again, I was stopped by Officer Blunt.

—He tried to break my goddamned TV, the bartender shouted from behind the bar.

—Is this true, Chief Joseph? I thought you were going to fight no more forever.

The police officer turned his head back to his partner. He did not see Chet reaching for one of the darts. Chet lifted it up, and jammed it through the back of Officer Poole's hand. The police officer screamed, holding his hand up in front of his face, not quite believing what his eyes were telling him. His hands reached to his utility belt, grabbed his nightstick, and swung it at my friend. The nightstick glanced off of Chet's skull. The skin split and blood poured out.

I rushed forward, but Officer Blunt grabbed me by the collar and pushed me out the door. I shouted to tell them Chet was a good man, that he would never hurt anybody. Blunt threw me on the sidewalk and ran back inside. I wiped blood from my split lip and listened to the thumps of the beating. I did not hear Chet cry out once. In a few minutes, more police officers arrived, their sirens like banshees, their cars jumping the curb and screeching to a halt on the sidewalk.

Fifteen minutes later, the paramedics arrived. They ran in with a yellow plastic stretcher. Ten minutes later, they walked out carrying Chet on top of it. The two of them could not carry the heavy man, so some of the police officers pitched in, including the red-haired officer who had started the beating, his injured hand wrapped in a bandage.

I cursed and pleaded and kicked at imaginary dirt on the ground, but no one paid attention to me. I waited for the ambulance and the rest of the cars to drive away, but I stayed outside for several hours, ignoring a meeting with Laura, neglecting my wife and daughter. When I finally headed home, it felt like a betrayal of Chet. He deserved a better friend than me.

19

I sat on my front porch, wondering how I would ever feel something else other than emptiness. My nerves were ragged from the events of three nights prior. They had scooped out something essential.

Near the curb, my daughter sat on her heels, drawing with chalk on the sidewalk. Any other day, I would tell her to be careful, to watch out for cars—even though few cars drove down our street. Today, I did not have the strength to worry.

—Come here, Eppy, I said.

When would I learn? I felt foolish every time I forgot about her deafness. This was not like forgetting a child's favorite color or favorite toy, although from the way children react when a parent forgets these, it would seem a betrayal for which forgiveness is impossible. By forgetting my daughter's deafness, it was as if I was forgetting I even had a daughter.

—I'm cheating on your mother, I told the air. —I've been cheating on your mother for a few weeks now, and I hope she catches me. Your mother needs to move on. She needs someone better. I drink more and more so she'll give up on me. She needs a man that she can look up to, to let her breathe. She needs a man and not whatever I am.

My daughter, of course, did not react.

—She deserves better than me. She deserves better than this town, that crappy museum. She deserves to be sipping espresso on a terrace in Florence. She deserves to be wooed by a billionaire art collector in a penthouse in Shanghai or Paris. I don't know.

Eppy drew and smacked her lips, oblivious to my words.

—You deserve better. You deserve a school with the budget to help you learn. A school that doesn't force you into a class with a boy like Darrin. A school that will listen to you when you say you're having trouble.

—This town isn't bad. No, it is a good town, but it is a town for me, not for your mother. She is different here and she will always be different. She is a novelty.

—Although you will feel sad when your mother and I divorce, remember that the pain will subside. Pain like that goes away. But don't forgive me. I want you to promise that you will never forgive me for what I did to your mother, what I did to you. It's better that way. None of this dual custody nonsense. None of this being shuffled back and forth between parents, trying to decide to whom you belong. You are your mother's daughter. Every good quality you have, you have gotten from her. Consider yourself lucky that you gained so few genes from me.

—I'm going to see Laura again tonight. I will try to see her every night I can until the truth comes out. I don't want to. She is sick and getting sicker by the day. She told me before the affair that she didn't want to be used. That is exactly what I'm doing. I'm using her to break up this marriage. I should be man enough to do that myself, to tell my wife that it is over, but I cannot, I am a child. Worse. A squid, a mass of jelly on the ocean floor, I am—

Eppy turned around. She had a smile so beautiful it could cleanse the darkest heart. Almost, I thought. Almost.

—Did you draw something? I asked her with a forced smile.

She smiled.

—What is it?

Don't see, Eppy signed.

I started to get up. She jumped forward, covering her drawing with her belly. She giggled and signed.

Don't see. It's not good.

I sighed. I started to feel better. If there were anybody who could fill this hole, it was her, but she wouldn't be around for much longer.

—Come here.

No, she signed. *You're just trying to trick me. As soon as I get up, you're going to run over here to look at it.*

—I won't.

Promise?

—Promise. Now come here.

She walked over and I put my arms around her. I wiped away the dirt off her snow pants and pulled dead leaves out of her hair.

—How was school? I asked. —Did Darrin give you trouble?

With a frown, Eppy nodded.

—I'll try to do something about that. I've got to do something. If Miss Black doesn't want to do anything, I'll complain to the principal. Don't worry. What happened? What did he do today?

When Miss Black went to get something from her car, Darrin chased me around the room. When Miss Black got back, he ran to his seat. I was still on the other side of the room. Miss Black yelled at me for being out of my chair.

—I'm sorry. I'll go to your school tomorrow. I'll make sure he gets in trouble.

Daddy, don't, she signed.

—Something has to change. I said. —The only thing you get for doing nothing is nothing.

Don't.

—You won't get in trouble. And if Miss Black treats you bad because of it, the school can fire her.

I don't want her to get fired.

—Don't you want a better teacher?

She's a good teacher. She thinks she knows more than she knows, but she's a good teacher.

—And what about Darrin?

Eppy shrugged.

—Don't you want him to stop doing the things he does?

She shrugged again.

It's hard to hate people.

This bit of wisdom struck me. I did not expect this from my daughter, or anyone her age.

—Most people I know find it very easy to hate other people. That's what makes you so spccial.

I learned that from you.

I gave one weak, emotion-choked laugh. The imagination on that girl.

I'm cold. Do you want to play inside?

—No dear. I have to go somewhere. When mom wakes from her nap, make sure she cooks you something to eat.

Do you really have to go?

—Yes, I lied.

Okay, but when you go, don't look at my drawing. It's not very good.

—I'm sure it is very good.

No. Promise. Don't look at it.

—Okay, I promise.

We hugged again and she kissed me on the forehead.

—I love you, Daddy.

After she had gone inside, I looked at my watch. Laura was already expecting me. She might be furious that I was late or she might be too sick to care. I hoped it was the former. I knew I should probably go inside, play with my daughter, maybe cook something up to serve my wife when she woke.

I got up and started toward Laura's place. I kept my promise, averting my eyes from Eppy's drawing as I walked past.

20

—Are you going to have to testify? Laura asked.

Laura sat on the floor of her apartment. I was half-dressed, staring down at her, or rather at the area that her voice came from in the pitch-dark room. We had tried to make love, but her coughing had interrupted us again. I hadn't performed again. Every time I looked at her, the sadness was a punch to the stomach.

—I am willing to, if asked. Please don't talk. Your lungs need rest.

—I need a new set of lungs is what I need.

Her voice was raspy and weak. Her disease had raged in the last couple of weeks.

—His family has a lawyer. He seems to think it is a pretty open and shut case of police brutality. One would think any jury would convict someone beating a man in a wheelchair half to death, but juries tend to go for cops and against natives.

—You see him?

—His family's very protective. I think more than one of them blames me for it. They'll probably be a little nicer to me once he gets out of the coma.

I did not say the word "if," but it hung between us like a tightrope. "'If" was a terrifying word.

—Sorry to hear about your job.

—Hell, I knew this "Winter List" was bull. If your mother told us she was selling the business and that the new owners only wanted half the workforce, well, we'd still be pissed but we wouldn't feel lied to.

—Mother was holding on the best she could. She was lying to herself, thinking she wouldn't have to sell. It hurt her a lot to let go of something she worked so hard at.

—I know that.

—She really needs the money.

—I know that too.

Laura coughed. I reached out and stroked her hair.

—Are you going back to the city? You could get your old job back.

—I never really had a job. I worked as an office contractor for years. I say contractor, but that is only a nice way of saying "temp." Companies don't hire anymore. They just work you for a couple of years for low wages, no paid holiday, no paid sick days, until you get a phone call saying they have made "the hardest decision" in their life and have to let you go. I'm sorry. I sound bitter but I just don't think I can face struggling to find an entry-level job only to lose it a year later.

Laura stood up. She pressed her hands against my knees as she stood up. Her joints popped and she wheezed.

When she opened the blinds, moonlight rushed in like water from a burst dam. She stood in front of the window, nude, not caring if someone saw her. She had lost a lot of weight in a small span of time. She smiled and struggled to suppress a cough.

—I'm going into the hospital soon.

Answering her would acknowledge that her statement was true, was the only thing that would make it true, and I did not want that. I couldn't wait forever.

—You can still have a transplant.

—I've been on the transplant list for three years. I'll likely be on it for three more. Besides, that would only give me a few extra years. It would be very expensive, and I don't want to leave my mother with that burden.

—What about the burden your mother would feel if you gave up?

I regretted saying it. How much pain has been unleashed on the world with just a few misspoken words?

—You have to have hope, I said.

—I hate hope. It keeps some people alive, but for those of us that are terminal it hurts so fucking hard. Hope lifts us up, only so we can fall farther. I want so much to live like a monk, happy for every moment I have left. But hope has its hooks in me. I wake up every morning and rush to the computer, searching for that article saying the cure has been found. Each day I don't have an attack, I hope that my body has finally learned to adapt. And then hope gives way, and I am destroyed, utterly. Sometimes I think that hope is the devil, gaining pleasure from my pain. Sometimes, I . . .

She trailed off into a coughing fit.

—Please don't talk, I said.

Laura went into the kitchen and poured herself a glass of water from a filtered jug. After her fit subsided, she smiled again.

—The dream of ending our relationship on an epic speech will have to be canceled, it seems.

—This is not the end of us.

—It is. I don't want you to visit me at the hospital. No, don't say anything. Don't plead, don't beg. I will already have to deal with mom. I will have to deal with those tears. I could not bear adding another set. I . . .

She broke off coughing.

—Please Laura, don't speak.

Laura had never been one to listen.

—I haven't been going to the office to work. I've actually been reading about quantum physics. In hope's last cruel twist, I convinced myself of some sort of miracle, that I'd somehow spring back to life in a thousand years' time, that people'd be able to reconstruct my DNA from nothing.

I sat in the moonlight. I thought about the universe and our brief lives. Billions of years ago, the atoms that made up Laura's body were forged by a star. That star went supernova, casting her molecules across the galaxy. Those molecules coalesced into the solar system. They waited in the Earth for billions of years, they traveled through the nuclei of amoebae, through the brains of the first amphibians that sought the shore. They traveled all that distance to form her. One day, all humans will die. One day, the Earth itself will die in a fiery inferno. But matter cannot be created or destroyed, only converted into energy, and energy can never be destroyed. Billions of years in the future, the energy that made up our bodies will stoke the furnace at the heart of another star. She had always been, and always would be, a part of this universe.

Laura looked at me, waiting for me to say something. I had the words ready, and if I could just give her some comfort, then maybe . . .

I said nothing.

Laura walked over and wrapped her arms around me in an embrace. She helped me get dressed again. I kissed her at the door, and then she closed the door on me forever. It was a long cold walk home.

How much pain has been unleashed on the world by saying nothing at all?

I stopped in front of my house and looked down at the sidewalk. At my feet was Eppy's chalk drawing, the one she had told me not to see. It was a drawing of a heart. Not the stylized Valentine heart of love, but the realistic heart of a human being. It was a good drawing, done in red with blue veins crisscrossing the muscle. Around it was a scribbled circle, a halo in yellow. I squatted down and touched the lines of her drawing. The heart is such an ugly thing, but what it creates is beyond anything I can name. It was only then that I realized that, before I left to see Laura, Eppy had told me she loved me. She used her voice, not her hands. I sat down on the concrete and sobbed.

Later that night, I stood in front of the bathroom

mirror. The door was open. On our bed, my wife snored deeply. I should have closed the door, as the light might have woken her, but closing the door might have, too. I had come in to shave. For what reason, I did not know. I felt the need to shave before I went to bed. I must have stared at myself in the mirror for twenty minutes. I realized how little I knew about myself. One eyebrow drooped a little below the other. A spot of redness, barely visible at the corner of my neck. Laura's lipstick? I confronted my true self, not the one built up in the mind, the one that glossed over imperfections, the one that consisted of the body as a whole being. It was strange to view this body and remember that it was not a whole being, but an impossibly intricate set of chemical bonds, a cloud of atoms on the order of magnitude of trillions of trillions. Does each cell know its existence as a part of the greater whole? Are they aware, say when a drop of blood is spilled, do the blood cells that still course through my veins know a part of their number has been lost. Does each cell think itself a complete being? Does the drop of blood on the city sidewalk curse its God as its protecting fluid dries up and is left only as a dark stain?

I looked down at the bathroom counter. In a glass, soaking in liquid, were my wife's dentures. She had not lost her teeth with age, but in one violent moment when she was nineteen years old. This thinking about blood on pavement reminded me of the story that my wife had told me about her assault on the streets of London. She was a freshman, attending Oxford University on a Rhodes scholarship. One day she traveled alone to London to take pictures of the royal buildings. As she was walking away from Buckingham Palace, several youths dragged her into an alley.

My wife did not tell me about her rape until after Eppy was born. This was after the first time my daughter's cochlear implant failed. The implant would fail two more times, her body rejecting the wiring that would allow her to hear normally. My wife cried briny tears, her windpipe holding itself shut against sorrow. I should have told her she was wrong, that it hadn't done something to her insides and caused Eppy's disability.

The men who had raped her were convicted and served sentences, albeit light ones. This was probably due to prejudice in the judge, thinking that a Middle Easterner walking on the streets and taking pictures of Buckingham Palace must have been up to no good.

Her attackers would have been out of prison now. Some might have continued their criminal lives, but I imagined at least one would have reformed. Perhaps he worked in an office. I imagined him calling home, talking in a gentle tone to his wife, telling her that he loved her and asking if she wanted anything from the store. I imagined him coming home, late at night. His work colleagues wanted to go out for drinks, and though he avoided drinking—after all, he had been drunk on that fateful day—peer pressure finally had its way. My wife's rapist drove home. Guilt burned in him for driving drunk but he couldn't take a cab home because he had to use the van the next day to take his children to the zoo. He went upstairs to his children's room and watched their sleeping heads from the doorway. Then, he went in and kissed his youngest daughter on the forehead. She awakened from her dreams and put her arms around my wife's rapist's neck and told him that she loved him. Afterwards, after saying that he loved her too, and that he was sorry for waking her, he went into his own bathroom and stared at himself.

Did he think of the day? Of course, he did. Did he remember the half-circle of my wife's teeth spread out in front of him? A voice crying out in a language he didn't understand, a voice that he knew was only pleading for him to stop, to let her live, but which only drove his anger?

I slept on the couch for three nights after my wife

revealed her rape. That was probably the worst thing I could have done. It was saying she was a dirty, damaged thing. I was saying that no man would want a woman who had been raped. On that fourth night, when I crawled back into our bed, her flesh twitched when I touched her. I apologized and made to get out. But she grabbed me and pulled me to her.

I heard a cough. I blinked and I was once again in front of the bathroom mirror. My wife was awake, but she didn't want me to know that. I turned off the light, undressed and then joined her in bed.

21

When someone asks me about my religion, I tell them that I am a devout atheist. This draws a laugh, as a man that believes devoutly in nothing is absurd. But it is true. I hold no agnosticism, no doubts. My atheism came around after a long process of deliberation, not a quick conversion from reading a Dawkins or Hitchens book. After turning the question over in my head, it was the only choice that made sense, or rather, the others could not be resolved without a lot of filler to make them make sense.

Still, as I was raised in a religious family that went to church more than once a week, religion was hard to forget. My formative years centered around Christianity, and I was at one time as devout a Christian as I am now an atheist. These old thoughts are still there, buried deep, and my newer thoughts have to tiptoe past them.

I would say that I am haunted by Christianity. My wife, as I have written, is a devout Muslim. I do not look down on her for this. I do not see her as naive or misguided, as some of my ilk are wont to do. I have tried to read the Quran, but never made it past the second or third sutra. From what I have read, I do know that Muslims believe in heaven and in hell.

That night, I had a dream that my wife and I were dead. In that dream, I was my wife and she was me. It doesn't make sense when I put words to page, but that is the strange, peculiar sort of somnomancy that dreams have. For this narrative, I will say that my wife was my wife, even though it felt like it was me behind her eyes.

My wife dies and she knows that I have died as well. Her eyes open to that great garden of heaven, under which rivers flow. It is a place of indescribable beauty, where everything is clean and sharp. Each tree a perfect tree, each rose a perfect rose. The amber light burns away all shadow, but is not harsh on the eyes. The garden is full of delights, full of anything she could desire. Except for one thing.

I am not there. She searches for me throughout heaven, even though she knows it is futile. The brooks splashing through the boulders, the birds singing the symphonies from the trees: these are all empty and hollow without the one she loves. This emptiness becomes the deepest pain, and since in heaven there can be no pain, it is not heaven.

One day, my wife sees a group of the resurrected in the garden. They are singing and holding hands as they walk down the verdant trail towards an amphitheater. My wife follows them. As she walks, she sees several more trails wending out of the hills. Throngs of the resurrected stride toward the same destination.

When my wife gets to the amphitheater, she joins in the crowd. At first, she can see nothing. She is too short. There are too many people. She asks a man to step aside. He obliges, although he does not take his eyes off the spectacle. Suddenly, my wife sees. In the center of the amphitheater is Tertullian's portal, that is, the portal through which those of heaven can see into hell, and partake in the pleasure of seeing their enemies burn there. The resurrected stare into the portal, their eyes hungry. They twist their lips into smiles.

My wife flees from the amphitheater and its grim portal. She is afraid she will see horrible things done to people through the portal. She is afraid that she will see me. She knows that one day someone who knew me and who hated me will go to that portal and my face will appear. She feels terror and terror is pain. It is not heaven.

My wife runs until her feet can take it no longer. When the stones cut through her feet, although there is no pain, red blood flows. Her lungs heave, even though she no longer needs air. She collapses at the back of an oak tree, heavy with blossom. Her eyes turn toward the sky. There is no longer a heaven to turn toward.

Then, from around the tree, I appear. I touch her hair and I caress her face. I tell her that I did not die an atheist, that I saw the light and that I declared that there was no God but God in my last breath, and that I was saved. I say that I have been looking for her for days, and have you been looking for me?

You look at me and start sobbing. I ask what is wrong, and you say that you know that I am not real, and that you know my last words, and they were not that. And even then, the holy book says those that convert on their deathbed do not get a reprieve. You say that this is an illusion, a trick, and that seeing this trick is more painful than if I were not there at all. You feel pain, and thus, it is not heaven.

After this, you feel the full light of God on you. You try to shield your eyes from Him, but you cannot. The light is so bright, you see your bones through your skin. And you feel God look upon you. You feel Him know you completely. You feel God raise you up, and reach into your heart to ease your pain. He raises you up with the other tortured souls, the ones who feel the loss of their loved ones that died not believing in Him, those that can find only horror in their enemies' pain; those who cannot believe the deathbed conversion. You feel His hand in your heart. He strips away all memories of me. It matters little how much I love you, He is too strong. He strips away memories of your father, your art. Everything in your life that could cause you any pain or sadness is ripped through your chest. Lastly, you feel God tug at the memory of your daughter. You hold on as long as you can, you hold on so hard, but He is so powerful. He is the meaning of power, the reason we can say that word. In the end, he takes her away.

It was here that I woke up. I lay in bed, staring at the ceiling, feeling lonely and lost and abandoned. I reached out, seeking my wife's hand in the darkness.

ABOUT THE AUTHOR

SHAENRAYCE LEIGLAND was born in Western Montana and attended the University of Montana. He currently resides in Alameda, California.